This Novel Is Dedicated to:
LADONNA MEDLEY
I Love You Best

CASH LOPEZ

By Barbie Scott

This is a work of fiction. All of the characters, organizations, and events portrayed in this novel are either product of the author's imagination or are used fictitiously. Any resemblance to actual persons, living or dead is purely coincidental.

Prologue

"Please Mario, I swear I don't know what he's talking about." Ross cried out for his life. Ross looked over at Jeco who wore a grin, and right then he knew Jeco was the one that told.

Ross had been the one dropping Liyah off to Papi's beach house were he lived with Pedro. Ross also found out Papi's true identity, because he was thanked by Pedro for always making sure Liyah was safe. He never told anyone of the discoverance and now he regretted it.

"I'm gonna ask you one more time Pendejo, where did you take my granddaughter?"

"I..I...please Mario..please."

Pop!

Mario sent a single shot, that pierced through Ross's nut sack.

"Arrrrrrr!" Ross cried out in pain.

"Next bullet is going to your cabeza." Mario spoke through clenched teeth.

"I..I.. dropped her off to the Lopez estate." Ross blurted out.

At just the mention of the name Lopez, Mario's eyes nearly popped out of his sockets. He walked closer to Ross so he could get a better understanding. There was no possible way there was life at the Lopez's mansion, so he figured Ross was a lying sack of shit.

"Stupid pendejo, I killed every mother fucker in that home so why would my child be there?"

"Be..bec..because she is in love with BJ."

"An who the hell is BJ?"

"Itss...Its..Its Cash Lopez's son. I swear I didn't find out until yesterday. Please man, I was just doing this for her. She was tired of…

Pop! Pop! Pop!

Mario sent two shots into Ross's chest and a third bullet into his head killing him instantly. Mario quickly walked out of his cellar in disgust. He proceeded to his limo and quickly hopped in to place a call. The moment the caller was online he tried his hardest to hold his composure.

"I'm going to ask you this, and, I'm going to ask you one time. When the ship blew up were there any survivors?"

"No sir. Not one."

"So why am I hearing that nearly 17 years later there are survivors? If this is true, *te voy a matarte*." Mario disconnected the line.

"Where to Boss?" The driver asked looking into the rearview mirror.

"The Lopez residence." he answered with a clenched jaw. The driver was stunned at his answer but wouldn't dare question Mario's instructions. He slowly pulled off and headed for the residence that once belonged to the most powerful woman in the world.

Havana Cuba...

Braxton looked at the beauty who laid peacefully on the oak colored sofa. She had been sleeping so peacefully he didn't want to interrupter her slumber. As bad as he wanted to let her enjoy her deep sleep, he knew that the information he had received could possibly change her life forever. He slowly walked over to her contemplating what to say. He looked through the glass walls of his home, getting lost into the waves that crashed against the shore. He sighed deeply then tapped her shoulder to awake her. When she finally turned towards him, her beautiful bedroom eyes made his heart melt like a ice cube on a summer day. At this point he wished he could forget all about the drama that lie ahead. He wanted to simply lay beside her, and hold her close to him. However, there were more important issues to deal with.

"Hey." she blushed shyly causing him to smile.

"Hey doll. I need you to get up and pay close attention to what I'm gonna tell you."

"What's wrong Braxton? You're scaring me."

"I want you to listen, and please listen carefully. I just received a call and the person told me that there were a few survivors on the ship." Braxton said looking into her eyes. The moment he said it, she became silent and it was like she had drifted to an unknown place.

“I don't know if its true baby, but I had to give you this information.”

“Wait how did you get that information?” she asked confused.

“I'm sorry I can't disclose that. But trust me, I have a gut feeling that its true.” Braxton dropped his head and felt horrible for the information he withheld.

“Oh my, Braxton, I have to go.” she lifted from the sofa in a frantic. She quickly ran to the bedroom that her and Braxton shared and began to pack a few items. At this point, packing a bag was the last thing on her mind so she grabbed the important necessities.

Before walking out the door, she looked back one last time. She wanted so bad to invite him along but she had to face this alone. She knew things could get hectic, and Braxton wasn't cut for outcome. He was innocent, and she didn't want to bring him any harm.

“I'll see you soon.” she told him with a secure smile. Braxton nodded with out a word and just like that, the love of his life had walked out the door to face what lie ahead.

Recap…

"You got me fucked up Brook!" Liyah screamed to the top of her lungs the moment they walked into Papi's mansion. "What you love that bitch? Huh? Thats yo new bitch?"

"Hell nah I don't love that bitch, but yes thats my new bitch Liyah. I mean what I'm suppose to do? Every Time you get mad you shake a nigga. I can't come to yo fucking house or nothing. That shit ain't cool ma." Papi was now screaming. Veins popped out his neck telling Liyah he was mad as hell. The roar from his voice was loud and demanding, it made Liyah jump.

"Whats going on down here?" Breelah approached the living area.

"My bad Aunty." Papi sighed. "Man she tripping." Papi looked over to his aunt.

"Oh I'm tripping? I swear you got me fucked up. Why did you bring me here in the first place. I asked you one single question. All you had to do was answer it and I would have left you alone for good."

"Its that easy for you huh?" Papi eyed her.

"What the fuck that suppose to mean? Nigga you the one got caught by yo little bitch while you was fucking her mother."

Liyah cried out. Papi rubbed his hands down his face, annoyed.

Bzzzzzz!

The sound of the buzzard caused everyone to look towards the intercom. "Who the fuck?" Papi asked himself with his eyebrows raised. He walked over to the nearest buzzard and pushed the intercom.

"Sup John?"

"Mr. Carter I have a young lady here to see you."

"Who is it?"

"What's your name mamm?" Papi heard John say to whomever the guest was.

"She says her name is Mo." Papi quickly shook his head and sighed out in frustration. The look Aaliyah wore let him know shit was about to get seriously real. Papi had grown tired of Aaliyah's childish ass ways.

"Man let her in." Papi sighed again then walked over to Liyah prepared for what was about to take place.

When Mo walked in, Breelah who had emerged from the kitchen eating an apple, was stuck in her tracks. Mo and Bree had an immediate stair down and couldn't believe their eyes. Mo just as everyone else thought

Breelah had died on the Yacht. Now she was nervous wondering who else survived the explosion. Breelah on the other hand wasn't to thrilled about Mo's presence. She knew all about "Moe the Hoe" as everyone called her. She knew every detail from Mo trying to ruin Cash's life and even her sleeping with Que.

"I know you not about to disrespect me Brooklyn!" Liyah screamed.

"Wait why is she here?" Breelah yelled as well. Papi looked over at his aunt, shocked at her demeanor. Breelah had began crying harder and everyone went into a frenzy. Wait, how the fuck she know where I stay. Papi thought to himself.

"Calm down Liyah damn. And Monique, how the fuck you know……" before he could finish the doorbell rang. Papi assumed it was John because they made it behind the gate. Because Breelah was closest to the door, she went to answer it. Papi knew he'd still have some explaining to do. When she opened the door she got the shock of her life. "Que?"

Chapter 1

"Its me in the flesh ma." Que stood there was a sexy grin. He was just as surprised as Breelah to be face to face with the woman he once loved. Breelah stood still with a shocked expression not knowing what to say. She knew Que wasn't dead because he wasn't on the Yacht, however, she thought they would never encounter again. An electric shock came rushing thru Bree's body. Nothing about him had changed except the small patch of gray hair that laid neatly on his chin. He was still sexy as hell all though he was now much older. Tears began to build up in her eyes and with out being able to control them, they began to fall freely down her face.

"Who is that TiTi?" Papi asked walking over to the door. He looked at the stranger in disbelief. He knew exactly who he was; Que.

"BJ?" Que asked also in disbelief. Though it was nearly seventeen years later, he knew BJ from anywhere. The scare over BJ's eye, and the long locks that BJ wore, was all the confirmation he needed.

Granted, Que knew what he did was wrong, he was happy as hell to know BJ was still alive. Looking at BJ made him feel close to Cash.

Everyday he beat himself up about what he had done, but nothing would bring his friends back.

"Que?" he heard a familiar voice. He looked past the young light skin beauty because he knew she wasn't familiar. When his eyes fell onto Monique, his eyes bucked and he raised one eyebrow.

"The fuck you doing here yo?" Que asked looking from Mo to Bree.

"Oh thats BJ's new girlfriend." Breelah smirked with a light chuckle.

"Damn yo old sack chasing ass still around. Let me guess, nephew got money?" Que rubbed his chin hairs.

"With all due respect, I'd appreciate if you watch how you talk to her." Papi came to Mo's defense. Aaliyah jumped into Papi's face ready to smack the taste out his mouth. She was tired of the disrespect.

"Forreal Brooklyn?" Liyah asked ready to tear up for the unteenth time tonight. She shook her head defeated, then did what she had been waiting to do. She removed the ring Papi had bought her and handed it to him. With one last look, she stormed out side leaving Papi in deep thoughts. He looked from Monique back towards the door and his heart told him to follow.

Papi ran outside to stop Aaliyah because he couldn't let her leave so upset. Que stood quietly because he didn't know what to say about the situation with BJ and Monique. He pushed it to the back of his mind, because something more interesting caught his attention. As he and Aaliyah crossed paths, it was something familiar about her. She looked like a split image of himself.

"Look, I think you should leave. He's dealing with a lot right now so I think its best." Breelah looked over at Monique. Mo who stood silent, wanted to say what was on her mind but she chose to remain quiet. She did as she was told and headed out the home. Right when Que began to speak, there was a commotion outdoors that made the two run outside quickly.

Making it to where the commotion was coming from, Que stood froze, as he locked eyes with Mario. Mario shot Que a grimsh look, and Que knew exactly what the look meant.

"Get in the car Mija." Mario gave order. Papi knew not to say one word to the man that raised Liyah so he stood quietly as Liyah made her way to the limo. Mario gave Que one last look then focused his attention to Papi.

"Stay away from my granddaughter. This is a final warning." the old man said and proceeded to walk to the car. Papi who wanted so bad to object, only shook his head. If it was up to him Mario wouldn't make it to the limo alive.

Papi was now upset so he stormed into his home. Que remained in the same spot dazed as he watched the limo pull off slowly. *That's my daughter. Damn she got big, and she pretty as ever.*

He thought feeling like a complete fool. Everyday Que thought of Aaliyah, and everyday he wished he could be in her life. But Mario made it clear, that if Que came anywhere near her, he was a dead man. Breelah played close attention to Que's demeanor. It was something about the way he looked that told her it was way more to the story. Brushing it off she walked into the home with Que hot on her tracks. It was time they had the conversation that Breelah been dreading for nearly seventeen years.

Chapter 2

Papi

As bad as Papi wanted to meet the infamous Que, rightnow his brain consumed so many thoughts, he couldn't focus. Aaliyah was mad at him, his aunt knew Monique, and by the looks of things, Que knew her all to well. Feeling foolish, Papi wondered if Monique knew of his identity this entire time. Tired of playing the guessing game, he made his way downstairs to where his aunt and Que were wrapped up in a heavy conversation. He knew how much Breelah loved Que so he was happy that they had reunited, however, he needed to get to the bottom of everything.

"How do yall know her?" Papi asked leaning against the fireplace in his living room. Breelah looked at Que as if she wasnt sure how to answer the question, so Que took it upon himself to speak up.

"The whole city of Miami know Monique BJ."

"Its Papi unc."

"Huh?" Que asked puzzled.

"My name is Papi so please don't call me BJ." Papi spoke seriously and Que nodded his head in approval.

"Aight Papi. well the bitch, done been around the block. I had her, yo pops had her, oh and let's not mention, her and yo moms was worst enemies. She used to work in Trap Gyrl as a barber until yo mom beat her ass and fired her. Look, I know you young and yes Mo is bad. Shit, she always been bad but that's where it stops. She ain't shit but a bag chaser. Trust me nephew she bad for business." Que spoke hoping Papi grasp everything he was saying.

Papi who was quiet, shook his head at the information. He felt played and betrayed because he had began to fall for Monique in a worst way.

"So where you been all this time?" Papi asked changing the subject. What he really wanted to ask, was, why wasnt he on the Yacht the day his parents were murdered.

"I been out the way raising my seed."

"So why you wasn't on the Yacht unc?" Papi asked bluntly.

"Shiddd." Que said shaking his head. He really didn't know how to answer the question so he chose his words wisely.

"Well for one, yo moms was mad at a nigga so I chose to not go. Breelah wasn't fucking with me either and that shit killed me." Que lied. "But check it, how yall been doing?" Que quickly changed subjects.

"We been good. Papi nodded. "Papa passed a few months back." a wave of sadness took over Papi.

"Papa?" Que asked in hopes he wasnt speaking of Nino.

"Pedro." Breelah jumped in.

"Damn is that right? Sorry to hear that. Pedro was my nigga. So who else survived? Que asked eagerly.

"Nobody really. Just me Pedro and TiTi. Who ever did that shit took my whole fucking fam." Papi spoke with vengeance. Every time he thought of the incident, he became furious. He looked at Que and studied the akword look he wore, but brushed it off. He so badly wanted to ask Que to help him find out who did this, but he chose to have that conversation at a later date. He knew that Breelah did not want this life for him. Hell, Breelah didn't even want him selling drugs, so a lot of things he would keep disclosed.

"Ima head to the shower." Papi said standing to his feet. He wanted to give the two some privacy. Papi headed to his room ready to get some shut eye. Looking at the time and realizing it was four in the morning, he knew he had a long day ahead of him. He had to meet with his connect and re-up on his product. He couldn't let the things going on in his life distract him from his business.

After a nice long shower, Papi laid in his king size bed and his thoughts were running like a wild bull. He wanted so bad to hop into his ride and go to Aaliyah's home. *Stay away from my granddaughter. This is a final warning.* Mario's words played over and over in his mind. A part of him wanted to kill Mario with his bare hands, then another part of him, wanted to fall back off Liyah. Last night, proved exactly what Monique always said; Aaliyah was a little girl that couldn't even leave the house.

Looking over at his dresser, the tickets to Liyah's prom laid on top of the bible his mother had for years. *Damn her prom coming up?* He thought to himself. He knew how much the prom meant to Liyah but he also knew her Papa wasnt having it. His mind began to drift off to visions of Aaliyah going to the prom with someone else. *I'll kill her and that nigga.* Papi thought getting angry with his own thoughts. He couldn't fathom the thoughts of his girl on the arm of another man. Though, he wasnt fucking with Liyah at the moment, she belonged to him. Finally coming up with a plan to surprise her at the prom, chill with her for a few hours then leave, he was able to relax.

Papi rolled over and began to browse his social media. He went straight to Aaliyah's page and began looking through her pictures. He then went to Moniques page and did the same. Before he knew it, he had drifted off into a deep slumber with his phone lying on his chest.

Chapter 3

Aaliyah

Aaliyah sat in her grandfather's study crying her eyes out. After the incident at Papi's, she went home and headed straight to her room. She was actually shocked Mario didn't chastise her, he simply let her go be in peace. It was something about the way her grandfather was acting that told Aaliyah something other than her relationship with Brooklyn had him in a rage. She decided to further investigate but right now she was dealing with heartbreak.

She couldn't believe Papi. The pain she felt was something indescribable. How could someone that proclaimed they *love* her, do her in such a way. Monique was an old, hoe, in Liyah's eyes and as bad as she wanted to dig up dirt on her, she left it alone. She was done with BJ for the last time, now she would focus on her education. The sound of the door creaking caused Aaliyah to become petrified. She knew it was her grandfather, but she was too scared to look up.

The moment she opened her eyes this am, he had summoned her to his private room and she knew it was about to be a chaotic scene.

When he walked fully into the room, he took a seat behind his wood grain desk. He looked at Liyah with much hatred that caused her to drop her head.

"How long have you been messing with that boy?" he asked burning a hole thru her.

"Umm...umm...a few months."

"A few months huh? An how do you know this kid?"

"I met him at school Apa."

"I see…" Mario spoke unmoved.

"Did you know that because of you Ross is now muerto?"

"Oh my…" Aaliyah covered her mouth with her hand. A second set of tears began to fill her eyes and she felt responsible.

"Noooo" she sobbed continuously. Her heart went out to Ross. Out of all the guards in her grandfather's entire empire Ross was the only one she loved dearly. Since a kid he was always so sweet to her. He would always go against his Boss's orders to please Liyah, and now because of her he was dead.

"But why Apa? Why do you have to be such an evil man." Aaliyah chose her words wisely.

"Ross was a good man. All he did was love me."

"He loved you?!" Mario shouted. "That Chingado don't give a shit about nothing but my fucking dinero" Mario roared.

"Yes!" Liyah jumped to her feet. "He loved me and matter fact he loved me more than you."

Aaliyah matched her grandfathers tone. She had never spoke to him in such a manner, but she wouldn't back down now. "My whole life you treated me like a fucking child."

"Watch your mouth!"

"No! No I won't watch my mouth. You've been keeping me here like a prisoner. I don't get to do the things my friends do and I hate it. Its always the negative things with you. So what I have a boyfriend! I get good grades and I'm not a bad kid!."

"You're right, you're not a bad kid and that's why I don't want you around that fucking Thug." Mario spoke meaning every word he said.

"Fine!" Aaliyah shot then stormed out of her grandfather's office.

When Aaliyah made it upstairs, she went to her bedroom to retrieve her phone but it was gone. She searched high and low for the device and it was nowhere to be found. If she hadn't found it soon she was gonna tell Blanca to get her another one. However, she prayed she didn't drop it in her grandfather's limo.

Flopping down on her bed, Aaliyah was emotionally drained. She was tired of the world and ready to give up on life itself. Her eyes roamed her room, and fell upon the exclusive dress that BJ had bought her for her upcoming prom. The way she was feeling at the moment, she didn't want to go.

She had no date and it would be an embarrassment to show up on the most important day of her life with out BJ. *Sigh!*

Aaliyah laid back and got lost within her own thoughts. For the remainder of the day, she remained cooped up in her room with her door locked, she didn't want to be bothered with anyone.

Chapter 4

Breelah

Its been three days since the encounter with Que and Breelah was on cloud nine. Seeing him brought back so many feelings and memories that she thought were buried along with her family. After that night, Que had been making it his business to pop up as if he had it like that. Granted he did, but Breelah would never admit to him that she was still deeply in love with him.

Breelah walked into the living room where Que sat watching television. She sat the tray down on the coffee table that consisted of a shrimp salad, a banana and a cold glass of apple juice. Que began to chuckle because Breelah complained about her body, when in fact she was perfectly fine. Over the last few days, Bree had caught Que up on her entire life. She told him about her occupation as an attorney and even a guy she messed with three years prior. Just the mention of another man in her life didn't sit to well with him, however, he couldn't be mad. He was living with not only one, but two women, and not to mention one woman had belonged to Bronx Carter, Breelah's now deceased brother.

Que watched Breelah as she finished up her salad. She left the room to take her bowl into the kitchen and he was now ready to have the talk he wanted to have. Once Breelah had appeared back into the room, she took a seat next to him. Que took it upon himself to grab Bree's hand, and she accepted shyly.

"What are we doing Que?" she asked unsure of what was now taking place.

"Ima be real ma. All these years a nigga never got over you. Not one day that went by I didn't think of you." he told her truthfully.

"But what does all this mean? I mean you have Keisha and your daughter in a whole other state and I can't go back down that road."

"You know, just like I know, that Keisha don't mean shit to me. Qui in college right now if that makes the situation any better. Bree, if I gotta show you I want you then I'll do so. I'll even move back to be with you."

"I don't know Que." Breelah twirled her fingers.

"Look, I'm not saying let's just rush into this, but in due time, I want that old thing back." he spoke sincerely. "Just tell me you'll give us a chance ma?" he asked and waited patiently for an answer. Breelah was so confused. she wanted to be loved but she knew Que was no good.

It had been years since Breelah was with someone genuinely. She missed the touch of a man, and truthfully, she missed Que's touch. But something was telling her dont spark old flames.

"Just give me some time." she spoke just above a whisper. Que nodded his head in respect. He couldn't say he didn't blame her.

Que stood to his feet and told Bree he would catch up with her later. They shared a simple peck and she walked him to the door. The moment he was out of eyesight, Breelah laid her head back on the wall and closed her eyes. Thoughts of Que consumed her mind and she felt confused. A part of her wanted to give him a chance, but the thoughts of knowing he had tried to kill her brother Bronx, clouded her judgment. For now she would go with the flow of things until her mind was made up.

Chapter 5

Papi

Papi swerved his Spyder in and out of traffic through the busy streets of Miami. He headed to Monique's salon because she had been blowing him up non stop. As much as he tried to avoid her, it was hard because she had grown on him. In a text message she told him to give her a chance to explain herself so he finally agreed. He also had a few things he wanted to get off his chest, which was the initial reason he agreed on the visit.

When Papi pulled up to the location, he quickly parked and hopped out his ride. He walked into the salon and noticed it wasnt as busy as usual. He figured because it was a sunday, business was gonna be slow, which was good just incase he had to kill the bitch right in her establishment.

"Hey Papi." Arcelie spoke flirtatiously. Papi didn't bother to speak back because he knew had Mo been around she wouldn't have been so friendly.

In mid stride, Papi stopped to watch Mo who was on the other side of the room behind a glass wall. He couldn't front if he tried, she was bad hands down. The white jeans she wore hugged every inch of her stacked frame. Her Tommy Hilfiger crop top showcased her belly button and on her feet she wore a pair of Tommy Hilfiger three inch heels. When she finally looked up, her and Papi locked eyes. Her eyes were pleading for Papi's forgiveness but he wasnt giving in so easily. He walked through the door with much confidence and took a seat in the empty chair that sat near the dryers. Monique was just finishing up with a client.

The client stood to her feet, payed Mo then headed out the door.

"Come on." Mo told Papi walking out the door.

"Where we going?" Papi asked with his face frowned.

"In my office." she replied then made her way through the salon.

"Celie could you lock the door on your way out." Celie nodded her yes and Mo walked into her office with Papi in tow.

"So what's so important you wanna talk about that got you blowing my phone up?"

"Damn hi to you too."

"Cut the shit ma. A nigga not here for no games." Papi said taking a seat. Mo leaned back on her desk making sure to face him as she began to speak.

"Look Papi, I'm sorry about everything that happened at the club. But you have to put yourself in my shoes. I was your date and here yo little bitch comes barging in. Then what you do? Leave with her. Do you know how that made me feel?" Mo was on the verge of crying.

"I understand all that. And I apologize Mo. but you know what it is with me and Liyah. And you also know your place in my life. But check it, when I first met you, I told you I didn't like easy around the block bitches. Which is one of the reasons I didn't take your daughter serious. Yet and still, not only am I hearing you fucked the whole Miami but you smashed my uncle Que and my pops." as the words left Papi's mouth, Mo dropped her head in embarrassment.

"Yes I slept with Que but I never had sex with your father Papi you have to believe me. And honestly, I was seeing your father first. He belonged to me and your mom went behind my back and started messing with him but I never smashed him." Monique spoke truthfully.

"Papi everybody has a past, everybody makes mistakes. No I'm not perfect and I beat myself up about it everyday. You just don't know what I've dealt with my whole life. Everyone judged me as if they were perfect. Nobody's perfect!" she began to sob. Papi watched her with a shocked expression because he hated to see a woman cry. He wanted so bad to comfort her but he wasn't done.

"Did you know who my parents were?" Papi asked the question that's been eating him alive.

"At first no. the first time we slept together was the day I saw the tattoos on your back. I swear before that I never knew."

Papi soaked up everything she had said and only nodded. Monique took it as her cue to walk over to him. For the last two days Monique had been dying inside with out Papi. Yes she saw dollar signs, but she genuinely loved him. All though Papi was over twenty years younger than her, he carried himself like a man, and even fucked her better than most grown men had her entire life.

Mo kneeled down in front of Papi and looked him in the eyes. His mind was telling him she was full of shit, but his dick and heart told him she was sincere. *Fuck what anybody gotta say. This my life and I run my own program.* were his thoughts.

"I love you. I know you may not believe me but I do. If you give me a chance, I'll show you." Monique said placing her hands on the top of his.

"If you rocking with me then you rocking with me. I don't wanna hear about another nigga ma. You not about to make me look like a fool out here."

"But what about…

"We done. A nigga ain't got time to be chasing no little girls." Papi spoke making Monique feel as if she won the race. Deep down inside he knew it was all a lie. He loved Aaliyah deeply, and unlike Monique, he couldn't give up on her that easy.

Monique placed a kiss on Papi's lips that made his dick rise in his jeans. Papi stood to his feet and began to undress.

"Take that shit off." he told Mo and she wasted no time.

Monique and Papi stood in Moniques office naked as the day they were born. There was so much fire between the two, they stood there gazing into each other's eyes. Breaking the stare down, Papi led Mo to her desk. In one swift move, he knocked everything down to the floor. Monique was so turned on, she didn't even care about the picture of Kamela that had hit the floor and shattered into a million pieces. Papi pulled Mo by one arm making her turn around. He wanted to hit it doggy style, and he already had plans to beat her lining away.

Papi began to slowly stroke himself. Not making her wait any longer, he slid every inch into her, going deep as he could. Mo screamed out in ecstasy as she tried to hide her smile. For the first time, Papi had went into her raw and she knew right then she had him where she wanted him. There was no turning back.

Chapter 6

Monique

Monique and Papi were so lost in the heat of their sexscapade, neither of the two had a care in the world. The salon was now closed and the only sound traveling thru the thin walls were the music that still played from the other side. Dej Loaf's Pandora played and the smooth sound of Tink's *Treat Me Like Somebody*, had Mo in a daze. The way Papi was hitting her box, she could tell he was beginning to fall for her. With every stroke, came a kiss and with every kiss was lust. As much as Mo told herself it was about the money, she had falling in love with his young ass as well. *This nigga really not wearing a condom.* She thought in the middle of the love making. As bad as she would love to trap Papi with a baby, her past was filled with skeletons that she knew would be awaken.

The night Que showed up to Papi's door, Monique's heart sank. Not because she once had a love affair with him, but because they bared a child she never told him was his. Kamela was in fact Que's daughter but she dared to ever confess. She knew that Que looked at her as some sort of hoe, so she didn't want to bother with the fact that Kamela was his child.

Now that she wanted to be upfront with Papi, she thought long and hard on telling him the truth. First she had to win him back, then she would tell Que.

Many days Kamela asked about her father and Mo would simply say he was dead. She had made up a lie about how he died during a robbery gone bad, so, Kamela would just leave the subject alone.

"If you make a fool out of me, I swear Ima body yo ass Mo." Papi whispered into her ear knocking her from her belligerent thoughts.

"I swear I won't baby. I swear." Mo cried out as he continued to thrust into her warm pussy.

"This pussy too good to share ma."

"Ohhh its yours baby. I promise its yours..ohh shit I'm about to...Im about too…" Mo could barely speak. Her legs began to vibrate and she was having a organism that took her to another place.

"Damn, yo shit like a waterfall." Papi bit his bottom lip on the verge of cuming himself. He quickly pulled out, and began stroking himself so he wouldn't bust already. He walked over to a chair and took a seat. He looked at Monique with the most lustful eyes and told her, "come ride this muthafucka." Mo wasted no time straddling him in the chair. She was faced forward, so as she rode him, he sucked her succulent breast one by one then two at a time. She used the tip of her toes to help guide her up and down.

"I love you Papi." Mo spoke so sincerely. She didn't expect him to reply but she had to let him know how she felt. Instead of Papi responding, he began kissing Monique with so much aggression. They both were breathing hard, they both were drenched in sweat, and today was the best sex they had encountered with each other since the first day in Mo's bed.

For the next two hours, Mo and Papi stayed cooped up inside of Mo's office. They went at each other like two lions in a pit. Nothing or no one could ruin the moment and Monique was happy because this was just what she needed.

"Bitch so what you gon do? I mean you have to tell him Mo."

"I am. But I have to tell Que first. A part of me want to say fuck it and remain quiet. Shit its been nineteen years. My baby don't give a fuck about no daddy.

"Yeah but truth be told she look just like his ass."

"Well If I keep her away from the nigga he won't know she look like him."

"I think you're making the situation worst. You made a promise to Papi, so being truthful is the best option."

"Ima tell him damn." Monique sighed in frustration. "Bye hoe, I'll see you when you get here." Mo told Arcelie then disconnected the line. The moment they disconnected, she had a call coming in from Papi. She smiled widely when she saw *My Baby* flash across the screen.

"Sup Ma?"

"Heyy Baby?"

"Shit just checking in on you."

"Awe you miss me?"

"I guess you could say that." he smirked on the other end.

"Asshole." she smiled causing Papi to laugh.

"Nah I miss you mama."

"Well when Ima see you?"

"I'll come get you in the morning. I got some shit I need to handle tonight." he lied.

Monique became slightly jealous but she wouldn't ruin the moment. Papi was a asshole at heart, and, a stubborn one at that, so she wouldn't dare get on his bad side.

"Papi can I ask you a question?"

"Nah ma no questions and shit." he laughed again. Monique ignored him and asked anyway.

"Are we official like a ref with a whistle?"

"We rocking ma, I told you that already."

"I don't know why, but I really hate that word." she pouted.

"Man stop pouting girl. I'm yours and you mines." he assured her. "Aight baby?" he asked making Mo smile.

"Yes babe I hear you."

"Aight then stop making me repeat myself. But check it, if I have time, Ima swing by the shop today and check in on you"

"Okay." she cooed into the receiver.

"Smooch." she said and again he chuckled.

"Smooch." he laughed and hung up the phone.

After hanging up, Monique was still in a daze. She thought long and hard and decided she would tell Papi about Kamela. She needed to be upfront with him because she didn't want anything getting in their way. Things were going great and he had confirmed they were official. So the best thing to do was tell him before he found out and things got ugly.

Chapter 7

Aaliyah

"Fuck that, Liyah, you gotta come. This is the day we've been waiting on for twelve years. Fuck Papi, you can't let him stop the most important day of your life."

"Yeah I guess you right. Its just, we had plans Venicia. We were supposed to be there together." Liyah whined.

"You and me both. Shit look at my situation, I'm pregnant by Cali and we still not going together. Man fuck them Bestfriend."

"How about we go together as each other's dates?" the girls laughed.

"Bet."

"So have you decided what you were gonna do?" Liyah asked concerned.

"Well a part of me want to just keep it. I finally told my mom and believe it or not she's excited."

"Your lucky. My Apa would kill me and the baby." Aaliyah joked but little did Venicia know, she was dead serious. Her grandfather was an old evil bastard and after the day he admitted to killing Ross, she wished he'd die a slow death.

"Yeah he foul. I can't believe he found out where you were." Aaliyah remained quiet because she would never tell the deep dark things she had known about her grandpa.

"Yeah that shit was so embarrassing. The hell with BJ and my grandpa. Let's go get our makeup done." Aaliyah quickly changed the subject. The two of them jumped into Aaliyah's car and headed to *Beat By Chas* to get their makeup done for tonight.

Walking into the prom, Aaliyah had butterflies. As much as she tried to smile, it was hard. Tonight was her special day so she wanted to forget all about BJ, therefore, she was gonna get drunk and have the time of her life. Aaliyah had a pint of Hennessy hid under her Pronovias prom gown. Venicia couldn't drink so tonight Liyah would be drinking the entire bottle alone.

Stepping into the main room, all eyes were on the dolls whom had just entered. Liyah's dress was flawless, her makeup was on point and her hair was laid and slayed. It didn't take a rocket scientist to know her dress was expensive. Papi had given her $5,000 for the dress and she spent every dime on it. Liyah began to fidget as she looked over to Venicia. Venicia also looked stunning in her Madison James gown that her mother payed for. The ladies were shutting prom down tonight and not one girl in the entire room could hold a candle next to them.

"Realize a lot of these niggas tell real lies" Venicia sang to lighten the mood.

"They not bout shit in real life, And that's something that I had to realize." Aaliyah joined in because this was now one of her favorite songs. The girls sung to the entire song as they made their way towards the punch table. Aaliyah wanted to grab a cup of punch to mix with her Hennessy so she wouldn't look to obvious.

"You look beautiful." Aaliyah heard a voice behind her. When she turned around, she came face to face with her ex, Timothy. She began to blush because she hadn't seen him in months.

"Thank you." Liyah beamed a wide smile. Timothy was looking good himself in a white tuxedo jackets and a pair of black slacks that matched the black rose in his right corner pocket.

"How did you get in here?" she asked curiously. Timothy was twenty-four so she was shocked to see he attended a high school prom.

"I knew you were here. I been missing you Liyah so I had to see you."

"Awe. that's sweet." she smiled taking a sip of her drink. Aaliyah and Timothy began to get lost into a deep conversation until they were interrupted by a arm nudge that Venicia had given her. When Aaliyah looked in the direction Venicia had pointed, her jaw dropped. Papi was standing at the entrance of the door scanning the room. *Shit!* Aaliyah cursed. Right then, his eyes met hers. The look on his face wasn't a pleasant one, so she assumed it had to be because Timothy stood by her side.

Chapter 8

Papi

When Papi's eyes fell onto Aaliyah, he had to admit, his baby looked good as hell. He studied her closely, and he now felt like shit. Him showing up tonight, reigned heavy on his mind for the entire week. He knew that if Monique found out she would die. But he couldn't let Liyah down. Suddenly, the smile that he wore proudly, was turned into a frown. He watched as Liyah's ex stood next to her. Papi's blood instantly began to boil. He went from zero to one hundred; quick. He walked over to the two and dared Timothy to say one word.

"Bring yo ass on so I can holla at you."

"For real BJ?"

"The fuck I say Liy Liy." he said letting her know he meant business. Aaliyah looked over at Timothy sympathetically. She knew BJ wasn't one to play with so she was gonna submit.

"I'm sorry Tim." she told him sincerely.

"The fuck you apologizing to him for?" Papi spoke furiously. Seeing that Timothy didn't want those problems, he grabbed Aaliyah by the arm and led her outside. At that moment, Papi hated he didn't have his gun on him, but he knew Timothy remembered the ass kicking he had given him a year ago.

Walking outside, the night air was slightly breezy. Aaliyah used her hands to clutch her shoulders. Sensing she was cold, Papi took off his suit coat and handed it to her.

"Thank you." Aaliyah spoke nervously. She eyed Papi up and down and damn was he looking good. She thought Tim looked nice, but he didn't have shit on her Papito.

"So that's your date?"

"No BJ." Aaliyah replied annoyed. *This nigga got his nerves.* She thought looking him in his eyes.

"You know you got some nerves. What, yo bitch somewhere sucking another dick? Is that why you here?"

"I came because I promised you I would. Look ma, I know I ain't perfect but I try. I love you to death and no matter what yo punk ass grandpa say, you gone always be mines. I never loved no bit…" Papi was cut off mid sentence as the sound of a car's tires came to a screeching halt. Before Papi could react, he was rushed from behind and hit upside his head with a metal object making him blackout. Aaliyah looked up from Papi and noticed Jeco standing there with a sinister grin. Upon orders, another guard swept Liyah off her feet and carried her over to the unmarked car. From the vehicle, she watched as Papi was dragged into a separate car. She began crying hysterically as she cried out. "Noooo".

In and out of a daze, Papi felt the car come to a complete stop. He couldn't make out where he was but something about the scenery told him it wasn't a good look. There were no cars in sight, and the huge brick building looked abandoned. Suddenly the door flew open and he was snatched out of the car. He was led into the building, and he was too dazed to put up a fight. Hot liquid pour from the back of his head soaking his dreads entirely. Touching the back of his head, he looked at his hand, and he knew it was in fact blood.

When he got into the dark building, he was led down a hall that smelled like piss and shit combined. The men led him into a dark room and placed him in a chair; cuffing him quickly. *This exactly why I keep my fucking strap. Fucking with her and this stupid as prom.* He thought angry at himself. The light came on and he nearly fainted. Aaliyah was chained up to a pole just like Jesus when he died on the cross. Next to her was a hispanic women that Papi had never seen in his life. Aaliyah weep silently but because she was gagged, her cries were muffled.

Once again he felt as if he failed her. The first time was when they had caught the gun case and now this. A part of him wished he had followed his first mind and stayed home with Monique but no, he just had to come. He watched Liyah tied to the poles, and he wanted badly to break down and cry. He knew it had something to do with Liyah's grandpa because he had seen the same guards before.

"I love you." Papi told her in hopes she believed him.

"Well ain't that sweet." a voice spoke sarcastically entering the room. Aaliyah's eyes grew wide not being able to believe her own grandfather was behind this.

"Man just let her go and kill me." Papi spoke in hopes.

"Oh I'm for sure gonna kill you. I warned you to stay away from her, but you're just like your hard headed ass mother; don't listen."

"Fuck you, you don't know my mother bitch."

"Oh now you really don't know who I am. Boy I'm the reason your pinche mother is dead. Your mother and her punk ass team couldn't fuck with me. I run Miami and I eliminate all my enemies. Ask Que." Mario began to laugh a sinister laugh.

"Fuck you!" Papi spat upset. He wished for one second he could get to the old man but he was chained down securely. Mario walked over to Aaliyah and looked at her shaking his head.

"Mija, you're already responsible for one death, now you're gonna be responsible for two." Mario lifted his gun and put a single bullet between Blanca's head. Aaliyah jumped from the sound of the gun then began sobbing more than before.

"You cross me, you die, its that simple. Just like Ross had disobeyed me, Blanca had done the same. Yes I found your little cell phone." Mario held the Iphone out for Liyah to see he indeed found it.

"I pulled the phone records, and imagine my surprise when I discovered it was in Blanca's name. Poor thing, I liked Blanca" Mario spoke walking over to Liyah.

"Now Mija, you know I forbid you to see this mutherfucker and you went against my orders. You have no idea who this pendejo is. Did you know you're in love with the son of the bitch that murdered your mother?" Mario asked taunting Liyah.

"You're a lying sick son of a bitch." Papi yelled out.

"I am the son of a bitch, but a Liar, No. You see, just how you're tied to this pole like Jesus Mija? This is just how his mother killed your mother." Mario said pacing back and forth. "Its either his life or yours, so, we're gonna do it like this. Either he kills you." Mario pointed to Liyah. "Or he kills himself. But first I have more things to tell you Mijo." Mario laughed then continued to taunt the two.

Chapter 9

The Beauty

She sat outside of the warehouse in deep thought. It was as if she was reliving her past life. Everything around her was like Dejavu. As bad as she tried to forget about everything in her past, it was something about the call Braxton had received that told her to find her way back home.

Her eyes began to build up with tears as she thought about the day her life had ended. All though she was still here in flesh, her heart, spirit and soul had died right along with her family and friends.

There's no woman in this world that could amount to you. This shit is till death, ma," Brooklyn said in a slurred tone.

Cash looked at him, and could tell everything he said was sincere. She was so caught up in the moment, she couldn't even respond. She kissed his soft lips before speaking, then...

BOOM!!!

Cash fell to the ground. Her body seemed to be in such a pain that it was indescribable. She didn't know what happened, but the feeling she was having made her wish it was all a dream. Blood began to cover her entire wedding gown. She tried her hardest to look around the yacht, and the first thing she spotted was the two bottles that laid next to her, that her and Brook had been drinking.

With much force, she began scanning the room. Brooklyn's body laid lifeless next to hers, covered in blood. His legs were missing and the sight before her was a horrible one. She began to cry harder for Brook and the pain she endured herself. Her eyes weakly scanned the entire boat, it was like everyone on the yacht was dead. Her mother laid lifeless, her friends laid lifeless, and even her dad was dead. The top of the boat was on fire and it seemed to be growing wider. Braylen was back inside sleep off medicine because of his teeth, and that pained her more that she couldn't get up to try and save him.

My baby, she cried out, thinking about BJ. she didn't see him and Pedro anywhere.

Maybe it was best she didn't because she knew that would be a horrific sight to see. Feeling defeated, Cash was ready to give up. She couldn't imagine life without her family. Her mother was all she had, she had just met her real father, and much worse she was only a mother for one year. For the first time in her life, she regret the life she lived. She knew that it couldn't be anyone but the Cartel that succeeded with such a stunt, and she also knew that a lot of this was behind Que and Carter. But the truth of the matter was, the Cartel had it out for her mother for many years now. Cash closed her eyes because she knew this was the end for her.

Heavenly Father, I come to you to ask for forgiveness. Please forgive me for all the sins I had committed in my lifetime. Please protect BJ's little soul if he makes it from this horrible tragedy. *She began to pray. Suddenly, she drifted into a dark place. She took her last breath because she wanted to join her mother, father, and husband. She felt as if there was nothing left on earth for her to live for, so she simply gave up.*

Suddenly, she felt hands moving briskly around her body. Next thing she knew, she was being lifted from the Yacht into a helicopter. When she made it to the hospital she was rushed into surgery for a blood transfusion because she had lost lots of blood. Her back was burned badly so she was heavily sedated to stop the pain, which made her fall into a coma.

One year later Cash finally opened her eyes. She looked around the unfamiliar room and everything around her seemed so peaceful. She had been having the worst dream of her life, however, it was her reality. Everyone she loved was now dead.

She tried to lift out the bed, but failed. She looked at her body and she was much smaller than before.

"Wooo let me help you with that." a stranger appeared from nowhere.

"Where am I? Who are you?" she asked question after question. The stranger sighed out

because he knew this would be a long night. For an entire year, he waited for the beauty to come too.

"Im Braxton, do you know who you are?"

"Yes I know who I am, and why you're talking to me like I'm some looney bin."

"Well you were in a pretty bad explosion. You were hurt badly. You've been in a coma for a year."

"A year? Oh my god?" she panicked "So where's my husband? Where's my mother?"

"I'm sorry but their all dead Ms. Lopez." right then it all began to come back to her. She remembered everything up until the prayer she said right before she died. Well at least she thought she died.

"So how did I get here?"

"When we flew you into the hospital, you had some really powerful people looking for you. They were trying to finish you off so I kidnapped you from the hospital."

"You did what? Oh my god are you crazy?"

"So what was I supposed to do let them kill you?"

"Yes..No..Oh my god." Cash began crying. "My poor son." she cried falling into Braxton's arms. After crying for sometime, she finally asked. "Where are we?"

"Cuba"

"Cuba?"

Chapter 10

Cash Lopez

The sound of another car door slamming broke Cash from her deep thought. She watched as the one man she had been wanting to kill for over twenty years, walked into the building as if he didn't have a care in the world. She had been following him for an entire day and this is where she was lead. *Its time.* She thought as she took a deep breath then exit the vehicle.

Making sure the coast was clear, she went into the same door she had saw him walk into. It was pitch black which was perfect because no one would ever see her coming. She pulled out her firearm that was equipped with a silencer. She crept up on the guard that was guarding the door, and before he could blink, she killed him instantly. She listened for sometime as the man spoke behind the door. Other than his voice, she heard the sound of a woman weeping. Suddenly she heard a single shot that caused her to duck. Realizing the shot had come from inside, she sighed in relief. "Fuck you!" she heard the sound of a young boy.

On the count of three, she slowly opened the door. She had a clear view of the inside and what she saw only caused more curiosity. There was a young girl tied to what appeared to be railing and another woman tied next to her. She saw the figure of a young boy who appeared to be tied to a chair. Another guard began to walk towards the door. With one single shot she sent a bullet that pierced him right between the eyes. *I still got it.* She thought as she walked further into the room. The sound of the man's body hitting the floor, made the man quickly turn around. When he noticed who the figure belonged to, his eyes widened with shock.

"Hello Mario." she spoke tauntingly.

"Bitch I killed you!" Mario spoke with much hatred.

"I guess you didn't succeed." she replied sending a bullet into his chest. He fell back dropping his gun and blood began to ooze from behind him. She walked over to his body that was sprawled out on the floor and stood over him. She cocked her head to one side, tauntingly.

"You bitch. I guess I'll see you in hell." Mario laughed a sinister laugh. Mario was a true soldier, so death was never a fear. He wasn't gonna beg for his life, because he wouldn't dare give her the satisfaction. He sucked it up, and knew now, it was his time to go.

"Nah bitch, I'm one of god's angels." she spoke as she sent another four shots into his chest then one to his head. She stood over Mario's body breathing hard. She wished she could have made him suffer, but she couldn't take the risk. She had been waiting years to send him to his maker and finally she got the opportunity.

"Mom?" the young boy spoke making Cash look over.

"BJ?" she asked as if her eyes were deceiving her. She ran over to him and hugged him so hard she hadn't even untied him.

Realizing he was tied up she quickly began to untie him.

"Oh my god BJ. Lord thank you. Oh my god." she was now crying. After seventeen years, Cash Lopez had finally reunited with her son. For the second time in BJ's life, he began to cry uncontrollably. Aaliyah watched from across the room and she was also crying. She was not only happy for BJ, but she was also happy the devil himself was now in hell where he belonged.

After the long intense hug, BJ broke the embrace and ran over to Aaliyah and began to untie her. The moment he pulled the gag from her mouth she began to cry out uncontrollably.

"I love you Brooklyn. Oh my god I love you." she broke free and jumped into his arm. Cash stood puzzled, but didn't bother to ask questions. Whoever the young girl was, she could tell they were in love, and she would save that conversation for later.

"Let's get out of here." Cash told the two and they headed out the warehouse relieved. Cash was over ecstatic, as she continued to thank god. Faith had brought her here today, and she would forever honor the man above.

"Mom stop crying." Papi looked over at his mother.

"I'm sorry BJ but you don't know how happy I am right now."

"Oh trust me I know." he spoke because he too was happy his mother was here in the flesh.

For so many years, he had wished for this dream to come true. He didn't know how to feel at the moment, but happy and relieved were the two of the many feelings. He was alive, Aaliyah was now safe, and most of all, he had his mother back in his life. *Thank you God.* BJ thought looking up into the sky

Pulling up to the Mansion, all the memories of the home caused Cash to cry all over again.

"Bj you sta…

"Yep. This all me ma." BJ finished her question then smiled at his mother. She couldn't help but smile, because he looked so much like Brooklyn. He still wore his hair in locks and looking over his appearance told her he was cocky just like Brooklyn.

The sound of Aaliyah's cries made Cash look to the back seat. She nearly forgot the child was there. She parked the car and turned in her seat to look behind her.

"I'm so sorry you had to see all of this. Where are your parents? I know their worried sick about you." Cash spoke sympathetically.

"That was my parents." Aaliyah spoke unmoved by Mario's death.

"Wait a minute. Mario….

"It was her grandpa ma. He raised her." BJ interrupted.

"So this means..Oh my god. I'm so sorry." Cash's heart went out to the little girl.

She witnessed Cash kill her grandfather and now Cash didn't know how to feel.

"Its okay Ms. Cash, he was really cruel to me. And I honestly believe he was going to kill me and BJ back there." Aaliyah said then looked out the window into the night.

"Wait are you two…" Cash asked putting two and two together.

"Yeah that's my girl."

"Was your girl." Aaliyah corrected him.

"Whatever girl. We'll talk about that later. But right now, let's get in the house and clean up."

"Yes. and once you guys are done, meet me outside by the waterfall." Cash told Aaliyah and BJ.

They all exited the car. BJ looked over at his mother with a goofy grin.

"Whattt?" she asked giggling along with him.

"Its a surprise." BJ smiled.

When they reached the door to the mansion, they walked into the house and made sure to shut and lock the door. After everything that had transpired tonight, they felt as if they were in a movie and their safety was at stake.

"BJ where the hell have you been? Boy I been worried sick about…." Before Breelah could finish, she was caught in her tracks. "Oh my god Cash! Please tell me I'm not dreaming. Please God wake me up."

"Its me Bree." Cash said running into Breelah's arms. The two held each other in their arms for what seemed like forever. They sobbed as they nearly squeezed the life out of one another. What felt like a dream, was in deed reality; Cash was back home in her kingdom.

Chapter 11

Breelah

"You two go get cleaned up while Cash and I have a talk." Breelah told BJ and Liyah. They both headed upstairs and Cash and Bree headed outside to the waterfall..

"Oh my god this brings back so many memories. All I could think about is my mom and Pedro sitting out here plotting." Cash said causing Breelah to slightly chuckle.

"Speaking of, Pedro just passed about six months ago."

"What? So he survived the ship?"

"Yep. he's the one who raised *Papi* as he calls himself."

"Oh boy." Cash chuckled.

"Yes girl. He gets mad when someone calls him BJ. but yeah Pedro raised him for all these years up until he died."

"How did he die?"

"Old age basically." Breelah nodded assuring Cash that he hadn't died behind the streets, and It made Cash feel a lot better.

"I just found BJ a few months ago. Him and Aaliyah had got into some trouble. He came to my office and girl I knew my nephew from anywhere."

"Hell yeah. That boy is a split imagine of Brooklyn." Cash said then looked out into the waterfall. She had fell into a trance, just thinking about her husband. All though she missed him dearly, she was ecstatic to have Breelah. It made her feel close to Brooklyn.

"So did your baby survive the explosion?" Cash looked down at her flat stomach. Breelah shook her head no and Cash was saddened by the news.

"So check this." Bree said changing the subject. "Guess who popped up at the door a week ago?"

"I'm scared to ask." Cash chuckled.

"Que." Breelah raised an eyebrow.

"What?!"

"Yes Cash. and for some reason he's been hanging around talking about getting back with me. I don't know. I mean that was so long ago."

"Shit why not? I mean he was the love of your life. I know the information about Bronx still interferes with you loving him but that was so many years ago. Gotta let it go Bree. Hell, we ain't gettin no younger." Cash hit her with a reassuring smile. "But check it, I have something I want to tell you."

"Oh boy." Breelah prepared herself for the information.

"Aaliyah is Que's daughter." Cash smirked.

"Oh my god you're lying."

"I wish I was. Tonight I killed Mario." Cash said making Bree clutch her mouth to keep from screaming out. "Yes he had kidnapped BJ and Aaliyah and had them in a warehouse chained up. I overheard him saying something about he warned BJ to stay away from his granddaughter but it didnt register at the moment. In the car I asked her where were her parents and she said Mario was her parent and he raised her."

"Wait a minute let's rewind this. The day Que popped up, Liyah was here. He was looking at her funny too. Then a old man came in a limo and went ballistic about her being here. After that, Que was acting weird."

"That's exactly why because not only was it her grandpa, but it was Mario our fucking enemy."

"So that's the sheriff girls daughter which was Mario's daughter?"

"Bingo."

"But why would he keep that from her is the question?" Breelah asked puzzled.

"You know, with Que, you never know. That nigg....Before Cash could finsh she was cut off.

"What yall old ladies out here plotting on?" BJ said coming from inside the house.

"Boy you been listening to your Papa too much." Cash said in reference to Pedro.

"Yeah he always told me stories about how him and my G Moms sat in front of the waterfall when they were plotting on something. I miss that old man." Papi also looked out into the waterfall. It was something about the waterfall that was tranquilizing. Anyone who sat there would go into a daze.

"So whats up Papi?" Cash smirked looking over at BJ.

"Come on don't call me that." BJ said embarrassed.

"Oh now its don't call you that. Yo ass sure did check the shit out of Que when he called you BJ." Breelah added.

"Man that nigga different." BJ said making the ladies laugh. BJ pulled out his phone and began to text.

Nephew: *Please don't tell her about Monique. Please TiTi*

Soon after, Breelah looked down at her phone, she tried so hard to contain her laugh.

"Speaking of the devil." Breelah played it off, as if it was Que texting her.

TiTi: *Ooh, what I want for this? (smirk face) I'm not gonna tell but you owe me a favor. I'll think of something.*

Nephew: *Lol that's fucked up but I got you. Nothing stupid though*

As soon as Breelah read the text she began laughing. Right on cue, Aaliyah emerged from in the house and looked over at BJ. As much as BJ tried to take his mind off tonight's tragedy, looking at Aaliyah reminded him of the horrific episode. He knew Aaliyah was going through it right now, so he would be here for her as long as she needed him.

"Hey Aaliyah." Cash gave her a warm smile. "I wanna speak with you." Cash patted the seat next to her. Aaliyah nodded and took the seat next to Cash. Papi went into the home to give the girls some privacy. Aaliyah began to fidget, afraid of what Cash would have to say.

"I just wanna tell you how sorry I am about your grandfather. I don't know if you know but your grandpa was a cruel man." Cash spoke and waited for Aaliyah to approve what she had just said. Aware of Mario's lifestyle, Liyah nodded her head in agreeance.

"Now what I saw today was unacceptable. I would never do such a thing to one of my kids, grandkids or anyone in my family. I know you may have heard things about me, but I'm a really sweet and nice person." Aaliyah looked at Cash and tears were pouring down her face. On the side of them, Breelah sat quietly as she took in everything Cash said. Cash continued.

"Now that your grandfather isn't here, me knowing Mario, he doesn't have any other family right? No wife or no kids right?"

"No ma'am."

"Okay so do you want to live in that house?" Cash asked unsure.

"Honestly Ms. Cash, I hate it there. Everyone is so mean to me. The only ones that loved me were Blanca and Ross and now they're dead." Liyah began to sob. Cash began to rub her back to assure her everything would be fine.

"She can stay with us Cash. That's if you don't mind me staying here now that your back."

"Of course not Bree. as much as I missed you guys, I'd love to have you and Aaliyah here. Would you like that sweetie?"

"Yes I'd love to. But what about BJ?"

"Let me deal with him." Cash pat her leg. I'm going to put your grandpa's mansion up for sale and put the money into an account for you. I'm also gonna rewire all his funds into the account so you should be fine."

"But how you're gonna do that. You have to be an authorized user."

"Girl you ain't heard about Cash Lopez? You better ask somebody." Cash playfully nudged Liyah's arm. The ladies laughed out and for the first time tonight, they all felt a sense of peace. Liyah felt so much better knowing she would be in the care of genuine people. She just hopped Papi wouldn't mind.

Chapter 12

Aaliyah

Aaliyah sat near the waterfall in deep thought, something she had been doing the last two days. It had been two days since the terrifying night, and everything replayed over and over in her mind. Through the nights she could barely sleep so she would go into the room with Cash and climb into the bed with her. Cash didnt mind because she knew Liyah was dealing with horrific things. And also this would give the two time to bond.

With Cash, Liyah felt safe. Her dreams were torture and she would wake up through the night crying. It was something about Cash, that Aaliyah loved. She seemed so sweet. For her to let Liyah live in the home, told Liyah she was in fact a sweet person. Granted, Liyah didn't know much about Cash Lopez, she knew Cash had a heart of gold. Plenty of times she had with BJ and his Papa and often listened to the stories Papa would tell about Cash. she heard nothing but great stories, and the stories alone made her feel as if she had been knowing Cash her entire life.

Liyah's mind drifted off to everything her grandfather had said that night. Most of it she didn't want to believe but some things stuck out like a sore thumb. *Do you know you're in love with the son of the bitch that murdered your mother?"* stuck out the most. She didn't know the truth behind it, but she would soon find out.

As Liyah sat watching the waterfall, tears cascaded down her angelic face. She couldn't believe the man that had raised her, her entire life would do such a horrible thing. For some reason she felt he was gonna kill her that night, and that's why she showed no sympathy when Cash murdered him. She knew her grandfather was a horrible, cold hearted man, but she never saw him act in such a way. It was as if his eyes had turned black, and a pair of horns came peeking out the top of his head.

Thoughts of Blancas lifeless body was etched in her mind. She knew that the thoughts would forever haunt her. She felt so bad as if it was all her fault. Had she not asked Blanca to buy her the phone, she would still be alive.

When Liyah walked back into the house, BJ was coming down the stairs dressed in some black jeans and a black Polo shirt. All though he kept it pretty simple, he looked good as hell to Liyah. She eyed him closely as he made his way down the full flight of stairs. When he reached the bottom, he looked at her and let out a silent sigh.

"Sup Stinka?" BJ spoke making Liyah's heart melt. She hadn't heard him call her that in a long time.

"Hey BJ." she smiled weakly.

"Let's talk." he told her and walked over to the sofa. The two took a seat and Liyah began first.

"I hope you don't mind me staying here?" she asked nervously.

"You good ma, I'm actually happy you here. So much shit going on around this bitch, I love having all three of the women I love in one house."

"So you still love me?"

"Hell yeah." BJ answered not missing a beat. "No matter what Liyah, Ima always love you ma. I know shit rocky right now, and soon, we gone get over this shit. So much going on, I could barely think right now. I need you to understand, you gone always have a place in my heart. This shit till death Liy Liy, just let me get my shit together aight?" *get yo shit together? Always have a place in my heart? Is this nigga breakin up with me? Wow, I knew he was gone chose that hoe over me.*

"Its not about no bitch ma. I'll never put a bitch before you." he spoke as if he was reading Liyah's mind.

"Where you going so early son?" Cash emerged from the kitchen.

"Umm..um I got some shit..I mean stuff to take care of." BJ lied. He looked over at Liyah and she saw right thru him. The look on his face, told her exactly where he was going. Liyah shook her head and ran upstairs as quickly as she could. Again BJ had crushed her into pieces.

Liyah figured after everything they had been through the other night, he would stay home and make things work between them. However, he left her to drown in her own sorrow, and she knew exactly where he was running; *to his old hoe.*

_Funeral

Aaliyah sat in the cremation parlor staring at Mario's ashes in a gold Vessel. She tried her hardest to pretend his death was affecting her; thank god she didnt have to try too hard. There was only a handful of people in attendance, because Mario didnt have much family. Either they were disowned or killed. There was about twenty guards, Ms. Campbell who cried her eyes out, a few cooks and maids, who attended the service. Mario had no friends, and even the people associated with him, hated him. Because Liyah was now over 18, she was his next to kin, so she chose to just cremate the body and get it over with.

Removing her dark shades, Liyah sat back and watched as Ms. Campbell screamed, yelled and fell out as if her and Mario were head over heels in love. Liyah knew her grandpa all too well, to know, that man didnt love no one.

After Ms. Campbell had gotten herself together, she looked over and noticed Liyah. Her eyes looked broken and her heart went out to a poor Liyah. She walked over and pulled her into an embrace. Liyah played right along with her as if she was truly hurt, and she was doing a good job acting.

"Liyah baby I'm so sorry. If you ever need anything I'm here for you okay?"

Aaliyah didn't say one word. She nodded her head in agreeance, as the fake tears fell from her eyes.

"Where are you living? Are you in that big house alone?" Ms. Campbell asked rubbing her shoulder.

"Well I have all the staff."

"Aww poor baby. You could always come stay with us if you'd like."

"Thank you Ms. Campbell." Liyah smiled.

After the service was over, the limo drove to the cemetery where Mario would be put into a wall. Liyah wanted no parts of his ashes and she sure didnt want to take them to Cash's home. Once they were done at the cemetery, Liyah headed to Mario's estate and began packing the important things that she wanted to take. After gathering her belongings, she went into Mario's room and began searching for anything of value. Aaliyah walked over to the safe, and opened it. Many of times, Mario had always told her about the emergency safe in his bedroom. It only contained, three hundred grand in cash, and plenty of expensive jewelry. Because Mario wasn't the flashy type, all he wore was expensive watches. The rest of the jewelry pretty much collected dust. After throwing all the jewelry into her handbag, she walked out of the room towards the door. The moment she stepped outside, she was met with the bright sun. Before stepping off the porch, she looked back into the home, and all the memories as a child came flashing back. For a moment she was in a zone, until she heard a voice that knocked her from her trance.

"Thank you for everything Senora." Angelo a young guard approached her. Angelo was only twenty years of age and he was the son of Blanca. One look at Angelo, and Liyah's heart was crushed. The poor child had no idea what had happened to his mother an Liyah wouldn't be the one to tell him. Now that she was selling the house, she had no idea what Angelo would do with himself. He had no family, except his mother who was now gone.

"Angelo where are you gonna go?" Liyah asked sadly.

"No se, no tengo familia." He spoke letting Liyah know he had no family. Liyah being the kind hearted person she was, she handed Angelo the duffle bag with the three hundred grand. When he opened the bag, his eyes grew wide as saucers. He looked at Liyah in disbelief.

"Gracias Senora." he shook her hand long and hard. He was ecstatic.

"Your welcome." Liyah smiled warm heartedly. She walked off towards her car and climbed in to leave. Once she was out of the gate, she looked back at the home as tears fell from her eyes. She used her hand to crucify herself, then blew a kiss into the air. This chapter of Liyah's life was now closed. She didnt know where the new road would take her, but she felt a sense of relief to finally leave the place that she considered torture.

Chapter 13

Papi

Papi drove down I-95 with so much on his mind. He was still ecstatic about his mother being home that he even cried every night. For the last two days, he had been cooped up in his room trying to grasp everything going on around him. He wanted to have a talk with his mother and find out where she'd been all this time but he chose to wait until she adjusted. Though she was trying to hold up, he could tell she was just astounded as him. Last night he heard her on the phone, and it was something about the call that had her weeping. He didn't want to seem as if he was prying in her personal life, so he stopped listening and went back to his room. He did hear her mention the name Braxton which made him wonder who was he. Something else was going on with her, because he peeped the way her and Breelah were acting. He brushed it off because he knew sooner or later he would find out.

Finally leaving the house, he had so much he needed to get done. First he had to catch up to Young so they could discuss the next drop then he would go holler at Mo. Thinking of Young, he hadn't mentioned to him that Cash was back but he knew he would have to tell him soon.

As much as BJ didn't want to leave Liyah, Mo had been blowing him up for the last few days. When she threatened to come over, he knew he couldn't let that happen. His mother would go ballistic so he chose to keep Monique a secret until things blew over. Knowing he was wrong for making things official with Monique, he couldn't help it. The day he had went to her salon, it was something about the tears that made her words seem genuine. He wasn't choosing Mo over Liyah, but he had gotten so accustomed to Liyah not being able to leave the house, it pushed him into the arms of Monique. A part of Papi was happy Liyah had moved in, because now he could watch her closely but another part of him knew chaos would soon follow.

Thoughts of the her standing next to Timothy at her prom still played repeatedly in his mind. He knew he was being selfish but Liyah was his and his only. The night her grandfather abducted them was another thing that weighed heavy on his mind. It was the things he said, that left him wondering. "*I'm the reason your pinche mother is dead now. Your mother and her punk ass team couldn't fuck with me. I run Miami and I eliminate all my enemies. Ask Que.*" is what he thought of constantly. He made a mental note to ask Young about it because maybe Young could help him understand.

When Papi pulled up to the Yacht his Papa had bought him, he walked on the dock and took a seat to wait for Young. This was their normal meeting spot because they trusted no one to be around while they discussed business. Young was the only person other than Kellz that Papi trusted. And the fact of the matter is, he trusted them most because his parents trusted them as well.

"Lil Nigga what's up?" Young asked walking up the stairs that led to the deck. Papi stood to his feet and gave him a manly hug followed by a pound.

"Sup my nigga. Yo I need to holla at you about some serious shit then we could discuss the shipment."

"Fasho."

"Man the other night Mario kidnapped me and Liyah."

"The fuck you mean he kidnapped yall? So where that nigga at now?" Young jumped up ready to go to war.

"He's dead." Papi spoke relieving Young.

"Peep though nigga, all this time, that's Aaliyah grandpa though. I mean I saw him a few times but I didn't know this was the same nigga that had murdered my parents. Peep this though. The nigga said *I'm the reason your pinche mother is dead now. Your mother and her punk ass team couldn't fuck with me. I run Miami and I eliminate all my enemies. Ask Que."*

"I don't know what he meant by that but that nigga Que had done some foul shit before. Que the one killed yo uncle Carter. Well at least that's what we thought. Carter had faked his death and come to find out Que was behind the hit. That's the reason he wasn't on that Yacht because him and yo moms was beefing over it."

"So you know the nigga back right?"

"Hell nah. I been trying hit that nigga for some work but he ain't been responding."

"Yeah he popped up at the crib the night of the grand opening."

"Word? I know yo aunty was happy as hell?"

"Hell yeah. She tryna act like she not but that nigga sho been coming thru a lot."

"Yeah that was his wifey. Que was a cold nigga. Shit yo aunty had slowed that nigga down though." they chuckled.

"Yeah he cool and all but its crazy because if Mario had so much beef with my G Moms and her crew why he didn't kill that nigga that night. Mario popped up to get Liyah the same night Que popped up."

"I mean shit Papi its prolly a lot of reasons. He prolly aint on that shit no more. That shit was nineteen years ago."

"But still Young, Beef like that don't just fade away. Que should have popped that nigga then." Papi looked out into the water. Something wasnt right and he would soon get to the bottom of it.

"I feel you but shit only time will tell. Just watch that nigga nephew."

"You know if I even sense some funny shit, Ima body his ass. My pops didn't like that nigga anyway." They laughed again as Papi spoke truthfully.

"Ima have a party on the Yacht next month. Ima give you all the details. And I got a surprise for you too."

"Strippers?" Young asked laughing.

"Nah this shit better than strippers. Its gonna be an all white party so make sure you dress for the occasion." Papi told Young smiling.

The two sat and talked for nearly two hours before finally leaving. They continued to discuss Que, Mario and the drop that needed to be made. Papi wanted so bad to tell Young about his mom's but that was the big surprise.

Walking into the salon, Papi knew he was in for a world of trouble. The look Arcelie wore confirmed just that. She wore a smirk that made Papi laugh out. He shook his head as he walked towards the wash bowl where Monique stood. He couldn't help himself, as he watched her in a sundress that made her ass clap every time she scrubbed the woman's hair. When he was in arm's reach, he slightly bent down and whispered into her ear.

"Ah nigga miss you Smooch." Mo slowly turned around. She wore a surprised look, that quickly faded to anger. She wanted so badly to smile but she couldn't give in. instead she put one hand on her hip and tilted her head to the side. Papi handed her the white roses that he held, but she acted as if she was still unfazed.

"Come on baby don't be like that." Papi tried to reason.

"Excuse me Elaine." she told her client and stepped into Papi's space.

"Let me finish my client and Ima holla at yo ass. Can you busy yourself around here or do you have to run off for another week?"

"Nah ma. I'll wait for you." Papi said as if he was a Romeo. Mo only smirked at him and turned around to attend to her client.

Papi wandered off around the salon bothering customers as he did normally. He then walked over to Arcelie and began to harass her.

"Celie you ready to let a nigga bend you over?" he laughed.

"Ooh you so disrespectful." she laughed as if she wasnt trying to do exactly that. However, she knew Papi was just joking so she laughed along with him.

"Nah I'm just fucking with you. But check it, which one you smashed, my dad or Que or both?"

"Un un.. Boy what's wrong with you?"

"I'm just asking because them niggas done smashed everything around here." Papi laughed out. Little did he know, Arcelie had indeed smashed both his dad, Que and even Kellz that no one knew of.

"Girl get yo boyfriend." Celie told Monique as she walked over.

"Papi leave people alone. You always bothering people in here."

"Man because yall boring as fuck around here. All yall do is stand around and do hair."

"Um it is a hair salon."

"Okay and liven this muthafucka up." Papi stated then pulled Monique onto his lap.

"I'm still mad at yo ass."

"Its cool. You won't be mad after we close and I bend that ass over yo desk."

"Oh hell no yall nasty." Arcelie laughed out.

"Girl shut yo peeking ass up. I saw you that day looking thru the glass before you left."

"Oh wow." Arcelie covered her mouth in embarrassment. Mo and Papi began laughing.

"Nah come outside though. I need to holla at you." Papi told Mo and stood to his feet. He walked outside and waited patiently for her to come to him. He leaned against his car and began to browse thru his phone. Of course he went straight to Liyah's facebook page. When he read her status he damn near lost it.

What's on your mind: *SINGLE with no worries!*

98 Likes 66 comments

Papi began to read comments and he really began to get upset. He couldn't wait to get home. He was gonna drag Liyah ass thru the house and not even Cash could save her.

Chapter 14

The Beauty

"Its been days since you woke up. Please eat something."

"I don't wanna eat, I wanna go home."

"Where you gonna go beautiful? Everyone back home is dead and those evil people would come after you. Please can you just chill."

"Chill? I'm in Cuba with a damn stranger. How I know you won't kill me?"

"If I was gonna kill you I would have killed you in your damn sleep. Do you know my life is on the line here. I left my damn job and not to mention the mother fuckers that's after you might be after me now!"

"Fine! Where's the damn food." I stormed into the kitchen. I was acting out stubbornly but little did I know I had actually hurt Braxton's feelings. I really didn't mean to, but this nigga had to understand. You don't just kidnap someone and fly them to Cuba.

After I was done eating, I couldn't lie, the food was amazing. Braxton knew how to cook which was good because I didn't plan too. I still hadn't transferred the money I had in secret accounts to Braxton's bank account. Truth of the matter is, I didn't know If I could trust him. A part of me wanted to trust this stranger, because he was right, if he wanted to kill me, I would have been dead.

I walked around the huge home to find him. I wanted to apologize but he was nowhere in sight. Finally after searching for him, I found him outside on the balcony. He was looking out into the water and I could tell something pained him. I stood at the entrance of the home and watched him closely. His sandy hair and almond skin tone made him look as if he was mixed with something. He stood about 6 feet and 2 inches. He had a nice muscular build which I assumed came from a consistent workout regimen. All though he wasn't the typical thug I was used too, he was incredibly stunning. I quickly shook the thoughts out my head and walked out onto the balcony to join him.

"You know I never wanted this for you. I knew who you were when you first came to the hospital. Hell everyone there knew who Cash Lopez was. I couldn't help it beautiful, one look at you and I was in love. I couldn't let them men harm you. I just couldn't." he spoke with out looking at me.

"I'm sorry Braxton. I just need time to grasp all this. I appreciate you saving my life but imagine how I feel. I lost my husband, my mother, my friends and most important, my child. I lost my step son also. A part of me don't wanna be alive. I want so bad to join my family." I began crying again.

"I understand. But I hate how you make me the enemy. You just don't know." he shook his head.

"For an entire year, I watched you in that coma and everyday I wished for you to wake up. I left my whole life in Miami. I had a girlfriend who I promised my love too. She wanted kids, I wanted kids, But no. I told her I had to leave on business and never went back. I left everything behind for you." he spoke so sincerely. I could tell that it pained him. I knew now, that he wasnt hurting because of his girlfriend, he was hurt because I was acting ungrateful. I walked over to him and wrapped my arm thru his. We both looked out into the water and got lost in our thoughts.

"I never imagined Cuba to be as beautiful. The only time I visit was to buy work when my father had run out." I laughed. "Its really beautiful here.

"Yeah. I've been here a few times on vacation. You know I always told myself one day I would live here. Who would have ever thought it would have been on these terms."

"I know right." I replied and laid my head on his shoulder. I couldn't help the peace that I felt with Braxton. I don't know where life would take me at this point but what I did know was, I would try my hardest to adjust.

Reality had finally hit me, that, there was no life for me back in Miami. I had no family, no friends, and not even my puppy. I knew somewhere Que was alive and one day I prayed we would cross paths. I know he thinks I'm mad at him because of the whole Carter thing, but truth be told, I needed someone in my life that I loved, so if it had to be Que, then so be it.

Chapter 15

Cash Lopez

"I'm so sorry ma'am he was in a meeting you could go back now. Down the long hall to the right" The lady at the front desk informed Cash.

"Thank you." she replied politely and smiled.

Cash looked around the restaurant and she had to admit, Kellz had the place well kept after so many years. A few things had changed but not much. Cash walked down the hallway knowing exactly the way. When she reached the door, she prepared herself for the outcome. She hadn't seen him in years and she didn't know how he would react. What she did know was, she was tired of crying but she also knew, the tears weren't done just yet. She still hadn't seen Que, nor Young but Breelah had informed her they were still in contact.

She pushed the door open and Kellz sat behind the desk fumbling through papers.

"Well hello Mr. Scott." Cash smiled. Kellz looked up from his work and the papers he held fell from his hands. He leaned his head back because he had already had an intense day. He thought his mind was playing tricks on him as he eyed Cash. Cash gave him time to grasp the encounter.

"You gotta be fucking shitting me." he spoke with so much confusion. He was happy, sad, confused. "Cash." he said almost in tears. He couldn't believe his eyes. Here she was after many years.

Kellz was so close to Nino, he had fell in love with Cash the first time he met her. Often he told Nino, Cash was the best thing that happened to him. Even during Nino's infidelity, he would always call him foolish.

"Its a long story. Do you have time?"

"Of course I have time for you. Man a nigga missed you so much Cash." he jumped from his seat to hug her.

"Where you been ma? What the fuck. This shit crazy." Kellz continuously shook his head. Cash studied Kellz appearance, and she had to admit, he was still handsome. His caramel skin was blemish free and the waves in his hair would make any girl sea sick. The vee neck tee he wore hugged his biceps incredibly. Knowing Kellz true age, he didn't look a day over twenty seven.

"Man you look really good ma." hc grabbed her shoulders to look her over. Cash simply smiled because she was thinking the same thing about him.

"You too Kellz. I see you been keeping up with the place." Cash looked around the office that once belonged to her husband.

"Yeah Papi little ass let me continue to run it. You know that boy is something else." they both shared a laugh.

"Yes he is." Cash spoke and began to fidget. She didn't know what to say at the moment because she was still in shock herself.

After the two caught up on where Cash had been, they began to discuss the situation with Mario. Cash had been so caught up into her and Kellz's conversation, she had lost track of time. She left the restaurant, and promised to be back soon.

When Cash got back home, she headed upstairs for a shower. After she was done, she placed a call that she had been dying to make. On the second ring, Braxton's musculant voice graced the phone, and she smiled.

"Hello?" he answered sounding exhausted.

"Heyyy.. you sound tired."

"Hey beautiful." he smiled at the sound of her voice. "I'm tired as hell. I've been working all day."

"Well maybe you should take off for a few days."

"No I'm fine. How's everything going out there?" Braxton quickly changed the subject.

He hated when Cash often told him he worked to hard. She didn't understand why he worked so much because they were rich. With the money Cash had in her accounts and the money Braxton had racked up, was enough to last a lifetime. Over the course of years, Braxton began working in Cuba as a private doctor. Because he was his own boss, he would be home enough to satisfy Cash, but at times he would work eighteen hours shifts.

"Everything is fine. You know some things I can't discuss over the phone so I'll give you all details when I come visit."

"Visit?" Braxton asked puzzled. "So you're considering moving out there again?"

"I don't know right now Braxton. Its really complicating. Where's Sklyar? Tell her hi okay. I have to go." Cash rushed him off the phone.

"Okay." he sighed and disconnected the line. Braxton on the other hand, had became slightly jealous. Because he never received confirmation to whom it was that was alive, he assumed it was Brooklyn still living after all. Cash on the other hand, was afraid to tell Braxton that it was her child who was still living because she didn't know how he would react to her moving back home. Cash had to be with BJ and Breelah and she knew the two would never agree to move to Cuba.

Cash laid back on her bed in deep thought. She looked over to the dresser and fell into a daze at the picture of her and Brook. Even after all the years that went by, she was still dying inside without him. She drifted off into space and thoughts of the first day she met him evated her mind.

"So, you own the place, huh?"

"Yeah, I do," I said in a low tone.

"That's what's up, Lil Mama."

"What's your name if you don't mind me asking?" I jumped straight to it.

"Nino..."

"No, I don't want yo street name that everybody calls you," I said, tilting my head to the side.

"Ha, why is that?" "Because, I believe when you like someone you're supposed to know the real them, and Nino ain't the real you."

"Oh, so you like me, huh?" he smiled.

"No, I don't." We both laughed and he playfully shoved me.

"It's Brooklyn, ma."

"Oh ok, Brooklyn, I like that."

"And, what's yours?"

"Cash..."

"Oh, it's cool for you to sweat me bout my government, but..."

"No, that's really my birth name, you wanna see my ID?"

"Yep!" he laughed.

"Cash dinner is ready." Breelah said walking into Cash's room.

"Im..Im sorry." Breelah tried to rush back out the door but Cash stopped her.

"Its okay hun. Come here I wanna talk to you." Breelah walked in and shut the door behind herself.

She took a seat next to Cash on the bed and crossed her legs to sit in an indian styled position.

“You miss him don't you?” Breelah asked sensing her sadness. She knew how much Cash loved her brother and she could imagine her pain because she too had lost the love of her life; or at least she thought.

“Yes. Its like no matter how long its been, he still crosses my mind. I miss him so much.” Cash tried her hardest to hold back her tears.

“I know you do but Cash you have to let go. Its been what 18, 19 years?” Breelah asked and Cash simply nodded.

“So you mean to tell me you haven't got no dick in that long?” Breelah chuckled making Cash smile.

“That's kind of what I wanna talk to you about. A part of me feels uncomfortable talking to you about this but I know you’ll understand. I spent these years living in Cuba. when the explosion happened, I was the only one with a pause when the EMT arrived. Well you too I guess.” they both laughed.

“So this handsome doctor kidnapped me and took me to live in Cuba. I was in a coma for an entire year. When I first woke up, I gave him a hard time. Eventually I gave in and got cool. We didn't have sex until about another year later. A bitch was horny.” again they both laughed.

“Now were together. He asked me to marry him a few times but because of Brooklyn, I can't

Bree." Cash began to cry. Her lips shivered and her heart hurt.

"Its okay. don't cry Cash please. I know you love my brother, but you have to move on sis. No matter who you fall in love with, Brooklyn knows how much you loved him. He can feel you Cash. he's with you in spirit. To be honest, I'm sure he's upset about you sitting here crying. You know he hated when you cried." Breelah nugged Cash's arm. When she saw the smile creep up on Cash's face, she felt much better.

"Thank you so much Breelah. I really needed that." Cash sighed in relief.

"So when we gonna meet this hunk of yours?"

"I don't know. He's still in Cuba and he wants me to come home. I haven't told him it was you and BJ who had survived the ship, so there's no telling what that man is thinking."

"Well I think its time you bring him around. You can't leave that poor man all the way out there Cash."

"Well that's the scary part. I know I can't because there's more." Cash looked at Breelah and swallowed the lump that formed in her throat.

"I have a daughter." Cash blurted out causing Breelah to clutch her mouth with her hand. The two got quiet and it seemed that they were lost for words.

Chapter 16

Que

Que pulled up to the Lopez estate ready for the talk with Breelah he had been dying to have. He gave her some time to get her mind right and he prayed she had. Growing impatient, he thought long and hard on rekindling the love they once shared. He needed his baby back and he would do anything to have her back in his life. For many years he thought about Bree and as much as he tried to shake the thoughts, he couldn't. Over the last few days, he had gone home to get his family back in order. As usual, he fucked the life out of Keisha, then laid in the arms of Gabriela for the rest of the night. Qui was now in college, and having her secure, helped ease his mind. His only problem now was Mario. He wanted so badly to kill him, he just had to find a way. Once Mario was out of the equation, he would get his daughter and him & Breelah could live happily ever after. His plan was to live in the Lopez mansion and constantly visit his two wives he had back home in Brazil. He knew the women wouldn't fall for his bullshit so easily, so he mustered up a plan.

Pulling into the home, he noticed an extra car parked in the driveway that he had never seen. His first thought was maybe Bree had a nigga over, but he quickly shook the thought off that maybe it was Papi who had purchased another car. Que couldn't front, Papi had grown into a man quickly and he liked his swagger. Though he looked like a split image of Nino, he still had an attitude like his mother. Thinking of Cash Lopez, pained his heart because he missed her sexy ass dearly. The guilt of blowing up the ship weighed heavy on his mind constantly but he told himself the milk was already spilled.

Walking up to the door, he rang the doorbell and waited patiently for Breelah to answer. After about three minutes, she finally emerged, but she wore a confused look Que couldn't read. She was drying her hands on a kitchen towel as she watched Que through the glass windows. Finally opening the door, she gave him a slight smile followed by a shy like blush.

"Sup sexy." Que smiled exposing the dimple that Breelah loved.

"Hey Que. what are you doing here?"

"Man you know what's up. A nigga been giving you some time to yourself. This time I won't take no for an answer." he stated walking into the home.

"What are you talking about?" she acted puzzled. However, she knew exactly what he meant.

"A nigga ain't got time for the games ma. I need you in my world baby girl." he gave her a pleading look. "You ready to make this shit official Bree?"

"Que you have to understand this is hard for me. Its been years and…." before she could finish, Cash emerged from the second floor. Que watched as she strolled down each step with ease. The long gown she wore made her look like an angel and her hair flowed with every step. *I gotta be dreaming.* He thought as he watched her take the last step.

"Hello Quintin." she called him by his government name.

"What the fuck yo?." Que said with a wide set of eyes. "I swear if this some kind of joke Imma beat both yall ass." he said and they all laughed in usion.

"No joke baby. Im home."

"Man you got a lot of fucking explaining to do." he grabbed her arm and pulled her in for a hug.

"I miss you too." Cash said smiling from ear to ear.

"Man who else alive?" he asked in a state of shock.

"Just me." Cash said and instantly became saddened.

"So where the hell you been ma?" he asked eagerly.

"Cuba." she smirked. "We need to talk about something." Cash told him changing the subject of her whereabouts. She then headed for the kitchen and Que and Breelah followed. the moment they reached the kitchen Cash began.

"We could talk about my whereabouts later. Right now I wanna talk to you about your daughter."

"Daughter?" Que played dumb.

"Yes. your daughter with Stephanie. She's here Que. she lives with us now."

"I didn't even know yo. Peep, the night I came here, Mario pulled up to get her. I swear I was checking her out and she looked just like a nigga." He shook his head. "So where Mario at because that nig…"

"He's dead." Cash blurted out. Que remained quiet trying to process the information. He wanted so bad to kill Mario himself, but he was relieved that someone had done it. His gut feeling told him that Cash was behind the killing, but he chose not to ask.

The moment he laid eyes on Cash, he knew with Mario being alive there was a possibility that she could find out about the explosion. Hearing that Mario was dead, was music to his ears.

"So who killed that nigga?"

"Look its a long story but right now I think you need to tell Aaliyah she's your daughter."

"I don't know man. She mi…." before he could finish, the look on Cash's face told him that someone was standing behind him. Building up enough courage, he turned to look behind him and Aaliyah stood there with tears cascading down her face. When Que tried to speak, she ran off.

"Damn!." he said feeling like shit. He didn't mean to hurt Liyah, but he just couldn't acknowledge her in the past. Mario had threaten to kill him the day Liyah was brought to him. Liyah was another one of the reason's Mario hated Que. Years ago he had sent his daughter Stephanie to seduce Que while in prison. The plan worked, until Stephanie fell in love with him. The affair lasted for quite a while, until Cash murdered Stephanie in retaliation. Liyah was left at the hospital, and when Mario was contacted, he took Liyah in and raised her. Que had never seen Liyah a day in his life until the day he showed up to the Lopez estate. All the times he had been to Mario's mansion, he prayed he'd see her but Mario made sure to keep her locked away.

"Ima go and talk to her." Cash said as she ran behind Liyah. Que shook his head and took a seat. He was so caught up in the moment, he didn't speak one word to Breelah. Breelah knew this was a heavy subject, so she left Que alone to think.

Chapter 17

Aaliyah

Aaliyah sat in her bedroom crying her eyes out. Everything around her was moving too fast. To fast for a sweet and innocent eighteen year old to cope with. So much had went on, that Liyah didn't understand half of it. She wasnt hip to the street life and she had no one to answer all the questions she needed answered.

The thoughts of having a father in her life did make her feel better, but she wouldn't speak so soon. She had heard her grandfather speak of Que many of times, which made everything so confusing. *Did he know he was my dad? Did my apa know he was my dad? Why didn't he love me like all daddy's love their daughters?* Were the few of many questions she asked herself.

She pulled out her phone ready to call her best friend. Before she could dial the number Cash walked in wearing an apologetic look. Liyah could tell that this situation was eating away at her but she couldn't fault Cash for not telling her. Cash stood by the window and looked out into the sky. Just looking at Cash, Liyah could tell that she was so broken. She had heard about Cash losing her husband, mother, friends and everyone else she loved and just the thought pained Liyah as well.

“For ten years I called another man father. The day he died, broke my heart into pieces. The love we had for each other was genuine. He payed attention to me even when my mother was to busy. One day, at twenty five years old, I overheard my mother and my drug connect arguing. They argued about me being his child and he wanted to confess but my mother didn't want him to. Neither of the two even knew I was standing there. I ran out of the house a broken woman and ran to the arms of your dad.” Cash chuckled with tears now running down her face.

“I cried my poor eyes out. I wouldn't speak to my mother for weeks. When she finally came and explained to me her reasons, I understood things a little more clearly. After so many years of watching everyone around me praise their fathers, I was happy to finally have mines. No matter how old I was, I was relieved to know who my real father was. The day everyone died on that ship, my father died along with them. After that tragic incident, I wished I had knew before because our time together was short lived.” Cash spoke with her eyes trained on the clouds. Liyah paid close attention to everything she spoke, and watching Cash cry only made her cry more. Liyah not only looked up to Cash as a woman or a great mother, she looked up to Cash as a hero. She had been dying for this day to come, and something told Liyah that one day, she would meet the infamous Cash Lopez.

"You know your grandpa had made enemies with lots of people. Im sure theres a reason Que hadn't been in your life. Now that you know he's your father, give him a chance because one day you might not have that chance to give." Cash spoke sincerely. Liyah nodded her head in agreement.

"Is he still here?" Liyah asked and Cash nodded her head yes.

"You know him and your aunt Breelah are working on rekindling their relationship. Girl your dad ain't gonna give up until he gets her back." they both laughed.

"Cash?" Aaliyah spoke above a whisper. Cash turned to face her, and the innocence in her big beautiful eyes, would make any human melt.

"Yes honey?"

"Thank you again for everything. I swear you make life worth living. Once upon a time, I hated my life. It felt like I was a prisoner. And just that fast you came and changed my whole world. When I first met BJ, all he talked about was you. Papa loved you so much he told us so many great things about you. When Papa talked about the explosion, I wished that I would one day meet you, even if it was in heaven" Liyah spoke truthfully.

"Girl you tryna make a thug cry." Cash cooed.

"I love you my new daughter. No one would ever take me away from you and BJ again. Now let's go so you could talk to your ratchet ass daddy. Girl that's another story Ima fill you in on one day." Cash smiled. When she seen the glow in Liyah's eyes, she felt more at ease. It was something about Liyah that Cash had fell in love with so soon. Liyah had reminded Cash of herself in so many ways. Her shy like demeanor, and also her sweet and innocent child like ways.

When the two made it downstairs, they walked into the kitchen where Que and Breelah where sitting at the counter. Liyah felt awkward because Que was staring at her as if he was studying her. He didn't speak one word but Liyah could see the regret in his eyes.

"I'm sorry about everything Liyah. Its a long ass story why I haven't been in your life. If you give me a chance to explain, I'll appreciate that." Que smiled.

Papi walked into the kitchen and everyone's eyes focused in on him.

"Damn why yall in this muthafucka looking sad and shit?" Papi said as he walked straight to the fridge like a starving teenager.

"Liyah is Que's daughter." Cash said looking at Papi for an reaction.

"That shit don't surprise me. Yall got all kind of twisted shit going on around here."

"Boy watch yo mouth." Cash told Papi. Papi chuckled then took a seat.

"My bad mom's a nigga gotta get used to you being around. But word? Thats crazy." he said looking from Liyah to Que. "she do got yo big ass head." Papi made everyone laugh again.

"Que you really the man round this muthafuck..I mean round here."

"Boyyy." Breelah laughed and playfully punched him in the arm.

"Lets let them talk." Cash said and everyone stood to leave the kitchen. Que sighed out loudly because he knew this was gonna be a very emotional subject.

Chapter 18

Cash Lopez
(A few days later)

Cash and Breelah walked into Papi's restaurant because the two had worked up an appetite. After a long day of shopping, they were starving. When they walked in, the lady at the front desk smiled politely and escorted them straight to a table. The host knew who Cash was but she wasn't so sure. However, just in case, she made sure to treat the two with courtesy. When they made it to their table, Cash began to browse the menu on the tablets they were provided . Nothing about the restaurant had changed and that made Cash happy. She was glad because Brooklyn had sentimentally built the establishment and even naming it after his mother.

Looking around the restaurant had brought back so many memories, and Cash tried her hardest not to cry.

"So, you come here a lot, I see" I picked up the tablet so I could browse through the menu.

"I guess you can say that," he replied with his eyebrow raised. He picked up the tablet that was in front of him. As he browsed the menu, a Caucasian guy in an expensive suit walked up with a nice

looking older lady and asked if they could take a pic with him. Now this was really weird. The situation had me wondering if I was dating some sort of celebrity.

"Mr. Carter, would you do me the pleasure of taking a photo with me and my wife?"

"I would love to, sir," Brook stood up. I sat back in my seat and smiled.

"Thank you so much, Mr. Carter. I love what you've done with the place," the guy said to Brook as he looked around the restaurant. That let me know why he was getting the special treatment. The minute he sat down, he picked up the menu. He must have felt me grilling his ass because he looked up from the menu and smiled.

"What, ma?"

"Nigga, you know what. So, you're the owner, huh?" He smiled again before responding.

"Yes, Cash."

"So, why you didn't tell me you were the owner?"

"Same reason you didn't tell me you were the owner of Juice," he said with a smirk on his face.

"Cash! Cash!" Breelah was screaming Cash's name.

"Oh hun...I'm sorry Bree."

"Girl you just zoned out on me."

"I tend to do that a lot." they both laughed.

Kellz came walking towards their table with a wide smile.

"Hey pretty ladies." he hugged Cash then reached over to hug Bree. "why y'all didn't tell me y'all were here?"

"Sorry Kellz. We didn't want to bother you."

"Man come on ma. This yo shit. I work for you." Kellz smiled a sexy grin. Cash couldn't help but admire Kellz. She didn't know if it was because he was still handsome, or because she was just happy to see old friends but he warmed her heart.

"If you ladies need anything I'll be in the office."

"Thank youuu." Cash smiled.

"Ohh Kellz sure is fine." Breelah nudged Cash's arm.

"Is he?" Cash asked acting unmoved.

"Yes he is. And he sure was eyeing yo ass." Breelah smirked.

"Oh my god Bree. That's Brooks friend."

"What that mean Cash? My brother is dead, Kellz is fine as hell and think about it, Kellz is the best candidate for you. Cash you can't trust no one out here but Kellz. You see what happened when yo ass tried to date Jah. nigga ended up being Mario's nephew."

"Your right ma, but I don't know. That's a little too close for comfort."

"Cash you can't be lonely forever. I know you have Braxton back at home, but that nigga ain't even you. You stayed around because you prolly felt you owe him your life." Breelah said making Cash ponder. Over the course of time, Cash had filled Bree in on Braxton. From his looks to his corneyness.

"I have to pee." Cash said standing from the table.

"Okay, do you know what you want?"

"Yeah just order me a lobster and some pasta." Cash smiled and headed to the ladies room.

After using the restroom, she walked out with so much on her mind. With out paying attention, she bumped into Kellz and nearly lost her balance.

"I'm sorry Kellz." she said as he grabbed her. It was something about the way he looked at her that made her feel slightly uncomfortable. Every since the day she had come visit, they had been talking to one another constantly but it was always friendly conversations.

"Its all good." again he hit her with his signature smile. "So what y'all getting into after this?"

"Well BJ aka Papi, wants to take us to Empire tonight." They both shared a laugh.

"Formally known as Juice." Kellz added and again they laughed. "Yeah that lil nigga was adamant about buying that place. You know you have a real life soldier on your hands."

"Tell em about it."

"Well ima slide through and fuck with y'all. Im bout to roll out. I already informed the staff that you were here so everything is on the house."

"Okay." Cash smiled. Her and Kellz stood in one spot momentarily and only gazed at each other. Finally breaking the stare down, Cash told him that she would see him later. She made her way back to the table and Breelah was taking a sip of her wine. When she noticed Cash, she looked up with a smirk but didn't say a word.

"Woooo I'm hungry." Cash was fidgeting. Breelah sat her glass down and hit Cash with another sly smirk.

"Whaaa?" Cash blushed.

"Nothing." Breelah said but Cash knew exactly what she was thinking. Cash didnt entertain her thoughts any further. After their food came, they talked, ate then left to get ready for the night.

Club Empire…

Walking through the club brought back so many memories. Some good, some bad but all in all, Cash had the best times in her establishment. She was actually happy BJ had purchased it because it held so much sentimental value. She tried her hardest not to cry, as thoughts of her and Brook played in her mind.

A single spot light came on and pointed directly onto me. I looked at DJ Bounce with a curious look on my face. He smiled and shook his arms as if he didn't know what was going on. When I turned around, Brooklyn was on one knee, he was holding what appeared to be at least 15 karats of diamonds. The ring was breathtaking. I looked into Brooklyn's pleading eyes as he proudly said the words, "will you marry me?" Now y'all know I'm an emotional thug so of course, I began to cry.

"Yes, Brooklyn, yes!" I shouted as if sooner or later, he would change his mind.

He slid the ring onto my finger, stood up, and gave the DJ a thumbs up.

Bounce shouted over the mic. "She said yes, y'all!"

Walking to the VIP section with Breelah in tow, like old times, Cash was shutting shit down. Today she had purchased a dress from Rich Addiction Boutique. The dress hugged every curve nicely and even exposed her plump breast. Every man her and Bree had walked by, practically drooled over the two beauties that crossed their paths. Before they made it to their section, they were stopped by a group of guys who had been gawking over them since they made it up the stairwell. *I still got it.* Cash smiled to herself.

"I wouldn't do that if I was you niggas." Papi emerged from nowhere.

"Awe Papi my bad my nigga, this you?"

"Don't matter nigga just keep it pushing before I put some hot lead in yo ass."

"BJ!" Cash nudged him. The guys walked off because they didn't want that issue with Papi. Not only was he the owner, but he had made a name for himself in the streets.

"Nah fuck that ma. You and Bree sit y'all hot ass down somewhere. Got these thirsty niggas all in y'all face"

"Boy don't make me beat yo ass in here."

"Beat my ass and Ima just catch me a body." he said with a smirk. Something about the way he said it, let Cash know there was some truth behind his statement. *This nigga is just like his daddy.* Cash thought shaking her head.

Taking a seat, Cash grabbed the bottle of Hennessy that the bottle girl had brought over. She poured herself and Breelah a drink, but something peaked Breelah's attention. When she looked in the direction that had Bree in a daze, she couldn't do shit but shake her head. Que was at the bottom of the club and he had to practically beat the women off him. When Breelah noticed him rejecting every woman that tried to flaunt themselves in front him, she couldn't hide her smile if she tried.

"I guess times have changed." Cash joked making Bree laugh out. Breelah grabbed the glass from Cash and quickly took a gulp. The two made themselves comfy and began to have their typical woman talk.

After a few hours of chilling in the club, Cash and Breelah were both intoxicated. Cash sat on the plush sofa as Que and Breelah danced like they were in a 1992 junior high school dance. Cash who wasnt done, reached over to pour herself another drink. Suddenly, the smell of expensive cologne filled her nostrils and the scent was all too familiar. When she looked up, Kellz had come into the section and took a seat besides her. "Hey." she spoke nervously. She didn't look at Kellz like that so she didn't understand why did she have butterflies. *Cash you can't trust no one out here but Kellz. You see what happened when yo ass tried to date Jah. nigga ended up being Mario's nephew.* She thought about what Bree had said earlier. She quickly shook the thoughts out her mind and awkwardly looked around the club.

"Ma you better go get yo daughter before I drag her out of here by her hair." BJ walked over looking like the hulk. His chest was heaving up and down, an whatever it was, Cash knew he was upset.

"What are you talking about BJ?"

"Liyah thot ass on the dance floor shaking her ass all on some nigga."

"BJ she is not your girl anymore. Leave that girl alone."

"Man fuck that ma. She disrespectful as fuck. Im telling you if you don't get her...." BJ was cut off because Liyah came storming into VIP.

"Have you lost yo damn mind grabbing on me like you crazy."

"Nah but you lost yours dancing all on that nigga like I'm not here."

"You not my nigga. Did you forget about yo old hoe you got home!" Liyah screamed in reference to Monique. Papi quickly looked at his mother out of fear, then focused his attention back on Liyah.

"Man take yo ass home Liy Liy."

"I ain't gotta go nowhere." Liyah folded her arms over one another. Cash looked around the club for Que and Breelah but they both had disappeared.

"Let's go Liyah. It's late anyway." Cash told Liyah hoping she would agree. "Did you drive?"

"No I caught an uber so I could drink."

"You prolly caught uber so you could leave with one of these niggas." BJ shot.

"Fuck you. I'm not you, hoe!" Liyah stormed off towards the exit.

"I'll take y'all if you need a ride." Kellz spoke up.

"Its okay Kellz. You just got here."

"I only came to fuck with y'all. So if you leavin I'm out too." Kellz said pulling his keys from his pockets.

"Ima gonna take Liyah home Papi. you be safe okay."

"I'm straight ma. I got a shit load of guards and two straps on each side of my hip." he told Cash as if everything was cool. *Oh Lord I've birth a monster.* She shook her head then placed a kiss on his cheek. She pulled out her phone and sent

Breelah a text that she was leaving. When she looked up, Kellz waited patiently by the exit. *Oh boy.*

Chapter 19

Cash Lopez

Pulling up to the mansion, the car ride was silent. Kellz appeared to be in deep thought and Aaliyah was in the back sound asleep. Cash couldn't help but laugh because tonight had looked like one of her old episodes.

Exiting the vehicle, she opened the back door to wake a sleeping Liyah. Her long hair was all over the place and and her cute pouty lips curled up as she lightly snored.

"Liyah. Honey wake up." Cash shook her a few times. Calling her name several more times, Cash knew right then she was overly drunk.

"Here let me carry her." Kellz said walking around the car. When he picked Liyah up, she still hadn't budged. She was knocked out cold.

"See this why you have to be 21 and over to drink." Cash and Kellz both snickered.

When they walked into the home, the house was extremely quiet. Breelah had text and told her she was about to leave the club but she was gonna spend the night with Que. BJ was still there so Cash pretty much had the house to herself. Kellz laid Liyah on the sofa as Cash went to retrieve a blanket from the cabinet. After getting Liyah settled in, Kellz headed to the fridge and grabbed himself a beer. He then made himself at home by going into the den to watch tv. Cash had went upstairs to take a quick shower so she left Kellz alone.

Staggering into the restroom, Cash bumped into every wall she had encountered. Because she was so intoxicated she chose to take a lukewarm shower afraid the steam would make her vomit. With the water running, she went into her room to strip from her clothing. Bumping into the dresser "ouch!" she screamed out in pain. Finally peeling out her clothes, she was so drunk she couldn't stop laughing at her own clumsiness.

"Cash you straight?" Kellz barged into the room. He didn't mean to stair so hard but he couldn't help his eyes. Cash stood fully naked and though she had gotten much older, her body was still to die for.

"Um..yeah.." she shyly grabbed her sheet and tried to cover herself up. "Im drunk." she laughed out.

"I see. Yo ass up here making a gang of noise." Kellz chuckled along with her.

The moment she took a step to head into the restroom, her feet got caught into the sheet making her stumble over. Kellz quickly ran to her side and scooped her up into his arms.

"Man let me help you before you kill yoself." he carried her into the restroom and placed her into the tub. Not wanting to leave her alone, he took a seat on the toilet and waited for her to soap up. After nearly thirty mins, Cash had finally got herself together and was prepared to get out. At this point she was too drunk to be embarrassed.

"Ima go make you some coffee." he told her then walked out.

Finally coming down the stairs, Cash had felt a little better but her head was spinning uncontrollably. She found Kellz inside the den and in front of him was the cup of coffee he had prepared for her. He was sitting on the couch with one arm above his head and the other on the remote. He was browsing through the television, as Cash took a seat next to him. Neither of the two said a word. Cash drunk her coffee quietly and Kellz had tuned in to an episode of Power. Once Cash was done with her coffee, she snuggled up under Kellz and began to drift off to sleep. "Thank you." she slightly whispered before she fell into a deep slumber.

Cash woke up the next morning and she couldn't believe she felt fine. This was one of the reasons she chose dark liquor over clear. Anytime she drunk clear liquor, she'd always wake up with a headache. When she opened her eyes, Kellz was gone and she was still laying on the sofa. The smell of his cologne lingered on the pillow and the smell was hypnotizing. Cash breath in a long hard breath to get a better smell. She closed her eyes to relive the moments of last night. The sound of her phone ringing on the coffee table broke her sensual moment. Looking at the caller ID, she smiled seeing it was Kellz.

“Hey.” she spoke half embarrassed.

“Sup sleepy head. How did you sleep?”

“Well I woke feeling great. So I guess good.”

“That's good. Yeah yo ass was knocked out, drooling all over a nigga.”

“Oh my god. I'm sorry.” she cooed making Kellz chuckle.

“Its all good. Well I went to get you some breakfast if you don't mind.”

“No thanks. I’m actually starving.” Cash rubbed her tummy as if he could see her through the phone.

“Aight I'll be back in a few.”

“Okay, thank you.” they disconnected the line.

Cash stared at the phone in deep thought. Her mind had to be playing tricks on her because she had these crazy butterflies every time Kellz was around. Last night she fell asleep snuggled on his lap. she was so comfortable in his arms, hell a little too comfortable. She didn't understand if the effect came from him making her feel close to Brook or what, but she did feel guilty about having those feelings.

“You and Unc sure looked cozy last night.” BJ smirked walking into the den.

"You just now bringing yo ass in this house?" Cash ignored him.

"Nah unc let me in like five this morning. I couldn't find my house keys."

"Its not like that. I was drunk and he made me some coffee. I guess I fell asleep."

"Yeah well by the looks of things you were very comfortable."

"Papi what you want? And why the hell you keep hurting that girl?" Cash quickly changed the subject.

"I don't know honestly." BJ said and took a seat. "Its like I got so used to her grandpa tripping. She couldn't never come outside or spend the night with me. That shit start getting on my nerves ma."

"That's understandable but she's here now BJ. you gonna miss her when the next nigga got her walking in the house the next day."

"She ain't stupid."

"Yeah okay."

"I wanted to ask you something though. Do you trust that nigga Que?" he looked at his mother with a stern look. Cash really didn't know how to answer the question so she remained silent until she gathered up the right words.

"Que has done some crazy ass things BJ. Most of the things he's done has been out of love for me. I know by now you've heard about the incident with him and your uncle Bronx?" Papi nodded his head yes. "Right, and that was because he was head over heels in love with me. No I don't agree with some of the things he's done, but I've come to the conclusion that a person would do the craziest things over love. Trust me. Your dad had me doing all types of things. I'm talking about killing, fighting, ready to run bitches over."

"Yeah I heard." they both shared a laugh.

"But why did you ask that?"

"No reason really. It's just something about that nigga. I don't know now, but I guess I'll leave it alone." Papi said and stood to his feet. Right then Kellz walked in holding two bags that contained white trays of food.

"Papi what's up nephew?"

"Sup unc." Papi spoke then shot his mother a smirk. Cash smirked back then dropped her head to avoid his eyes.

"I'm about to go shower ma. Then Ima go holla at my boy Cali."

"Didn't yo ass just get here? You think you slick Papi. what yo ass doing in them streets?"

"Nothing woman. I'm just living." he said and quickly walked out. Cash knew it was more than just living. She couldn't quite put her finger on it but BJ was up to something.

Chapter 20

Papi

Papi stood in the kitchen of Monique’s condo cooking up his work. Monique busied herself around the house, moving from room to room as she cleaned. She had her boo there and her music was going, she was in a great mood.

Kamela walked into the kitchen in a pair of boy shorts and a tank top. Papi looked over her body and no lie, her shit was stacked. *She think she slick.* He chuckled to himself. He turned his head and focused on the contents in his jar, but that only made Kamela annoyed. Smacking her lips she turned to Papi.

“what's so funny?” she asked walking over to where he stood.

“You, thats whats funny. You need to put some clothes on yo.”

“Why? You know you miss this.” she smirked.

“You wild shawty.” Papi chuckled.

“Put some damn clothes on!” Mo yelled walking into the kitchen. Kamela rolled her eyes at her mother and before she walked out, she hit her with a sly.

“I ain't got nothin he ain't seen already.” she smirked then headed into her room. Monique grabbed her forehead as if she had a headache and sighed out. She was about tired of Kamela and her shade. Everytime Papi was around she had some slick shit to say. Lately the two hadn't been seeing eye to eye. They barely spoke and constantly argued. Kamela was jealous of the relationship that Mo and Papi had, because Papi would never wife her. Kamela asked herself over and over, what did Papi see in her mother, because she was just as much as the hoe he constantly referred to her as.

Papi finished up his last bit of work then grabbed his ringing phone. When he saw it was Cali, he told Monique to get the door. Cali didn't want to come in, trying his hardest to avoid Kamela, but he had no choice because Papi was cleaning up the mess that he had made.

Moments later, Cali walked into the kitchen and dapped Papi.

"Nigga where yo ass been?" Cali asked because his homie had been kind of distant.

"Man so much been going on." Papi shook his head. He didn't mention to Cali that his mother was back home safe and sound. At times he thought about telling him, but he knew Cali would tell Young and he wanted it to be a surprise.

"Where the fuck you been, I know you been seeing me call yo phone?" Kamela asked walking into the kitchen. She now had on a pair of sweats but she made sure to keep on the crop top that exposed her flat stomach and tits.

"Man don't start that shit Mela." Cali said already annoyed.

"You prolly been with yo ex bitch." she shot making him even more annoyed.

"Man ain't nobody been with that girl." Cali lied.

Every since Venicia told him she was pregnant, he had been doing everything in his power to get her back.

"Yeah that's what yo mouth say."

"A Papi Ima be outside in the car." Cali said then headed out the door. Papi laughed because Kamela was too much. He couldn't understand why she was pretending to be head over heels over Cali when in fact he could hit again if he wanted to.

After Papi was completely done, he grabbed his keys and headed out. Before he left, he told Monique he would catch up with her later. He knew she was gonna be upset because he had promised to take her to eat. He didn't intentionally mean to break his promise but cooking his work took longer than he expected.

After driving around for a few hours distributing his work to his traps, Papi headed back towards Monique's home. In mid stride, his phone rang and he pulled it from his pocket. Looking at the caller ID, he smiled. It was Camery a little cute redbone he had met in his club. Camery wasnt the normal thick that he was used to, but she was really pretty and had a nice petite frame. All though he had promised himself to Monique, *what she didn't know wouldn't hurt*, was what he always said. And if she did find out, he would hit her with *Im young ma. My dick thinks for me sometimes.*

Laughing at his on stupidity, Papi answered the phone with a sly smirk.

"Sup sexy?"

"Hey Papi." he could hear her smile through the phone. Just thinking about her pretty smile and perfect teeth had Papi feeling jittery inside.

"Shit just got off work." he lied. He wouldn't dare tell any woman what he did for a living. Most of them always asked what he did to get money but he would never admit. Because of the fancy cars and his lifestyle, everyone assumed he was a dboy. He would simply say his parents owned a law firm and he worked as a paralegal.

"Oh okay. Well I was hoping I could see you?"

"Is that right? You ready to let me bend that shit over huh?"

"Oh my. Nooo. I just met you dang can we go on a date or two first."

Date? This bitch think this is? Dates are for relationships. He thought as he moved the phone from his ear to look at it.

"Where you tryna go?" he asked half interested.

Fuck it. I gotta take her to eat for the pussy then thats what Ima do.

"Umm. don't matter. Somewhere on the beach perhaps."

"Aight. Text me your address and I'm on my way."

"Okay." she replied anxiously then quickly hung up.

Pulling up to the restaurant of Camery's choice, Papi actually enjoyed the ride. The two had talked about all types of things that Papi would have never thought would hold his interest. What intrigued him the most, was the story about her being in the military. She had been there for four years and that alone was exciting to him. He asked her about shooting guns and killing, and to his surprise, she had actually killed. She named nearly every gun ever made but when she pulled a gold Titanium Desert Eagle from her purse, he fell in love. Papi was infatuated with guns thanks to the pool house his Papa once occupied at the mansion. When his Papa passed, he informed Papi there were over one hundred firearms in his home. True to his word, Papi discovered them upon his arrival.

Walking into the restaurant Papi held the small of Camery's back. Since the whole gun talk, he had actually got in tune with his date. He had showed little more interest, and the thought of smashing was no longer at the top of his *to do list*.

Because it was a sunday, the restaurant was pretty packed so they agreed to sit at the bar. Papi didn't mind because he actually wanted a couple shots of Remy Martin. Upon taking their seats, him and Camery began to finish their conversation. Papi made a mental note to keep her around, however he prayed her pussy matched her personality.

Chapter 21

Monique

Walking through the mall, Monique and Arcelie laughed because every man they walked past tried to talk to them, and every woman shot them dirty looks. They went from store to store and basically bought out the mall. They made their way to Gucci which would be the last store they shopped in. Mo wanted to buy Papi a few belts and a couple pair of shades. She loved when he wore his designer shades. After making a few purchases, they headed out of the store ready to call it a day. They had spent numerous of hours inside of the mall and they both were exhausted.

On the way out, something very interesting peaked Mo's attention making her nudge Arcelie who was busy scrolling through her phone.

"Damn you get around little mama?" Monique smirked.

"Bitch don't worry about me. Old hoe" Liyah spat.

"Damn Que you fucking her too?" Monique and Celie laughed out.

"Man shut yo hoe ass up. This my fucking daughter you dumb bitch!" Que shot ready to beat her ass right there in the mall.

"Daughter?" Monique asked confused

"Yeah bitch his daughter." Liyah snickered. Monique was so taken back by the information, she stood still with a shocked expression.

Que and Liyah laughed in her face then made their way into the mall.

"Wow thats crazy. You think they lying?" Celie asked not believing what she had heard.

"Hell no. that girl look just like him."

"Yeah and she lowkey look like Kamela to Mo. Mela just a bit darker."

"Hell yeah they look alike." Mo said still applauded by the news.

When the two got into Mo's Bentley, they were quiet. Mo was still caught up over the news about Liyah being Ques daughter and Celie wasnt making shit any better.

"You need to tell them Mo. shit getting deeper and deeper ma."

"Celie please don't start. I said Ima tell them." Mo was annoyed.

"When? When its too late? Papi and Que gone beat yo ass."

"They ain't gon do shit." Mo snarled. Celie could tell she was annoyed so she kept quiet for the remainder of the ride.

When they pulled up to Celie's home, they didn't say another word to each other. Monique couldn't wait until she got out the car. The moment she grabbed her bags and closed the door, Mo sped off burning rubber off the block.

Instead of going home, Monique decided to grab a bite to eat. Driving along the highway, her song come on the radio. She turned up the music and began to sing the lyrics of SZA *The Weekend.*

"You say you got a girl, And how you want me, How you want me when you got a girl? The feeling' is wreckless, Of knowin' you're selfish, Knowin' I'm desperate." Monique was busy singing her heart out.

After the song went off, she played it one more time. The song reminded her of when her and Papi had first hooked up. However, she went from his weekend chick to his 9-5.

Pulling up to *StripSteaks,* Mo couldnt wait to get her hands on a juicy steak. She was hungry as hell and she refused to wait for Papi.

She parked her car and made her way inside.

"Hello welcome to Stripsteaks are you dinning in or out?"

"Hi. I'm doing takeout."

"Okay well would you like to sit at the bar and wait for your order?"

"Sure, can I get a menu."

"Sure." The host handed her a menu.

Monique headed for the bar. Before she could get fully in view, her blood began to boil. Papi was sitting at the bar with some chick. What pissed her off, was, he looked mighty cozy with her and the smile on his face told Mo he was enjoying her company. She looked the girl over and she wasnt a threat. However, she was extremely pretty and young.

Monique walked over and slid into the seat next to the two. She flagged the bartender over and ordered a glass of Ciroc. Papi looked over at the sound of her voice. When he noticed it was Mo, he sighed and shook his head. Camery looked at him and she sensed something was wrong.

"Hi Im Monique and you are?" Camery shot Mo a confused look then looked at Papi puzzled before answering.

"I'm Camery." she smiled. "Do you guys no each other?"

"Well Im his girlfriend but since he's here with you I guess I'm not." Monique shot Papi an evil glare.

"Come on ma. We just chilling."

"Looks to me like its more than chilling. Especially since her hand is on your leg."

"We are just...."

"I didn't ask you to speak Camille."

"Its Camery."

"Who gives a fuck."she waved Camery off. "Papi so this what we doing?" Monique now looked heart broken.

"I just told you we was chilling Mo."

"Well this chilling session need to end now before I mop the floor with this hoe."

Camery's neck nearly popped out of place but she held her composure. Camery wasnt one to have altercations with women because she knew her capabilities. Other than just shooting, she also knew how to fight; Monique wouldn't stand a chance.

"Look Mo, just go home ma. I'll be there in a minute."

"Nigga Im not leaving here with out you. So let's go so we could drop her off."

"Forreal Monique? Man you bugging."

"Im bugging? But you're here on a fucking date."

"Come on Camery let me take you home ma."

"Papi if you get up to attend to this bitch I swear its gonna be issues."

"Man you ain't gone do shit. Go home NOW!" Papi shouted in Mo's face.

Monique grabbed her purse from the bar and stormed out the restaurant. When she reached her car, she couldn't believe that she had actually started crying. She couldn't believe he had the audacity to take up for the chick. She sat in car and watched as Papi and his little friend exit the restaurant and hop into Papi's car. A part of her wanted to follow behind, but she knew better. She started her car and drove home in anger. She now hated the fact that she let Papi young ass make her fall in love. Now what she had forgotten, was, Papi was the son of Brooklyn Nino, and to the Carters, hoes came a dime a dozen.

Chapter 22

Aaliyah

"Aaliyah casually spent around in her black *House of CB* bodycon dress to get a better view of her back side. The dress fit every last curve to a perfection. Her hair was in a messy bun so she chose her diamond earrings to complement the hair doo. Grabbing her rolex watch and her Carolyn Crocodile clutch purse, she headed downstairs. Tonight she was gonna teach Papi a lesson by going on a date. She was tired of sitting in the house with a broken heart.

Liyah had met a guy inside of Papi's club. She didn't want to seem like some sort of hoe, but it was something about him that intrigued her. He was a bit on the square side but the way his pants slightly sagged, she knew he had a little thug in him. His baby face, cute dimple and his neatly bladed waves, was a completely different look from Papi. Dont get it twisted, Papi was the sexist thing alive to Liyah. His tall muscular frame and his long locks were to die for. Papi had a cute baby face but his full body tattoos made him look older. The scar above his eye, gave his baby face a dangerous look that intrigued her.

"Ohh check baby out." Cash told Liyah making her blush. Liyah did a slight spin to let Cash check her out.

"I need his name, social, address and phone number." Cash told her half serious.

"Mommyyyy." Liyah whined.

"I'm just playing baby. But I do want his phone number. And before yall pull off Ima make sure the security cameras get a shot of his license plate."

"Okay." Liyah chuckled shyly.

"So where y'all going?"

"I don't know, just out to eat."

"Okay well you enjoy yourself and be safe. You got your gun?"

"Yesss." Liyah chuckled again.

"I'm just making sure." Cash smiled widely.

Right then, their was a knock on the door. Liyah opened it nervously, but quickly released her breath when she saw that it was Kellz.

"Where you going Liy Liy?" Kellz asked looking over her appearance.

"On a date." Liyah smirked hoping he pass the word.

"Date?" with who? And do Papi know you dressed like that?"

"Papi who?" Liyah smiled making Cash laugh. However, Kellz didn't see anything funny.

"Leave that girl alone. BJ is doing BJ so she can do what she wants."

"Oh so you in cahoots with this shit?" Kellz asked looking over to Cash. Before she could reply, the doorbell rang and Liyah began to fidget. Cash quickly opened the door, before Kellz got a chance to antagonize the poor kid. Liyah stood back as Cash introduced herself. He introduced himself politely then was invited into the home. When he stepped in, Cash looked him over then mouth the words "he's fine." also hitting her with okay sign. Cedric was dressed up nicely from head to toe. His cologne had Liyah caught up in a trance.

"Let's go Cedric." Liyah started feeling uncomfortable. While Kellz eyed Cedric, Cash made a mental note to ask what he did for a living. She could tell his clothes were expensive, but not only that, the jewelry he wore was bright enough to light up the entire mansion. He wore a pinky ring, a lengthy cuban link and a very expensive watch. The diamonds in his ears looked like skittles and his *C* pendent was covered in diamonds.

"You guys have a great time." Cash rushed the two out of the home. Not only was she scared Kellz was gonna say something out of the ordinary, she didn't want to take the chance of Papi showing up.

"So tell me a few things about yourself ma? Like why yo sexy ass ain't got a boyfriend?" Cedric asked taking a sip of his Ciroc. Aaliyah couldn't help but smile. He was sexy as hell and had a beautiful smile.

"Well I just wanna graduate. I really don't have time for a boyfriend."

"Well I hope you make time for me. I'm feeling the shit out of you and I'm willing to wait for you if I have to. No rush baby."

"Awe." Liyah cooed shyly. "That's sweet. And yes we could see where this goes." she blushed.

"Thats whats up. So what do you enjoy doing? Like outside activities."

"Well I really haven't did anything out in the world." Aaliyah picked at her food. She thought about her Apa and how he kept her captive. She never got a chance to do what teenagers done."

"What you mean by that?"

"Well my parents are wealthy, so when I would ask could we go horse riding, they bought me a damn horse. When I asked to go to K1 Speed to ride bumper cars, they put a track in the yard. You get what I'm saying?" Cedric burst out into laughter.

"Thats dope as shit though." he was still smiling.

"What do you enjoy doing?"

"Well I enjoy music, I sing. Other than that I like to ride dirt bikes and shit. That shit be having my adrenaline pumping."

"Oh my, be careful on those things." Liyah spoke.

"So you don't do anything illegal do you?" she asked unsurely. Cedric lightly chuckled and wiped his mouth with the table napkin.

"Nah ma. Don't judge me because the way I dress or the fact that I'll kill a muthafucka." he laughed making Liyah laugh with him.

"I'm straight by the board. Your folks ain't the only one with loot ma. I was raised well off, so I never had to do anything illegal. I got a legit 9-5. Even though I go to work when I feel like it, but I do have a job."

"Okay you mentioned it to me on the phone but I thought you were just a spoiled kid."

"Yeah I'm spoiled as hell but I get my own dough."

"I like that." Liyah smiled.

"So you ready for me to get you home ma?"

"You tryna get rid of me already?"

"Ha ha ha. Nah ma. I just wanna respect your wishing on taking it slow. Now if you wanna come back to the crib your more than welcome." he chuckled making Liyah smirk.

"Nah I'm just fucking with you. But for real Aaliyah, I really like you so Ima do whatever I could do to get you. And if that means being a total gentlemen, call me poindexter." again he laughed.

The two got up and headed to Cedric's 2017 Challenger. As they walked to the car, Cedric couldn't help but eye her. She was the prettiest girl in the world to him and he meant what he said about waiting for her.

Cedric drove Aaliyah home just as he promised. Not only did he want to be respectful towards Liyah, but he also wanted to make a great impression to her parents. Cash was extremely nice but it was something about Kellz demeanor that wasnt sitting well with him. Assuming Kellz was Aaliyah's father, he didn't want to get on his bad side.

Chapter 23

The Beauty

One Year later….

Waking up from the horrible dream I had been having since the day of my wedding, my bed was drenched with sweat. My face was stained with tears, due to me crying in my sleep. Everything had felt so real, as if I was reliving the explosion.

I lifted from the bed because I couldn't go back to sleep. I walked into Braxton's room and when I saw how peaceful he looked as he slept, I couldn't help but admire him. He was laying on his stomach with his arms under his pillow. Because he wasnt wearing a shirt, the structure of his perfectly sculptured body was arousing.

For the entire year that I'd been here, I was finally adapting. It was hard coping with the fact I had lost my whole world on that ship, but it was time I moved on. No matter how many tears I shed, nor how many times I asked god to bring my family back, they were all dead. I knew it was selfish of me to wish I had just died with them, because my mother had always told me never question God's plan.

Climbing into the bed with Braxton, he began to stir in his sleep. I snuggled up under him because the fear of my dreams had me shook. I wanted to feel safe. I needed to be protected, so here I was cuddling with Braxton. The moment I was comfortable, I closed my eyes and drifted off to sleep.

4:40 am

I woke up out my sleep. Again I was having a dream, but this time it was more intense. Brooklyn and I were making love on a cloud. The way he made love to me, felt like heaven literally. "Cash." Brooklyn called out to me, but his voice sounded different. "Cash." I heard him call out to me again, but his mouth wasnt moving. Finally my eyes fluttered open, and I stared into the sexy face of Braxton. My pussy was drenched and I was sure I had caused a puddle in the bed. Braxton watched me, but didn't say a word. For quite some time, we both laid there.

"Make love to me Braxton." I moaned out. He gave me an unsure look but when he saw I was serious, he began to slowly remove my clothing. He was so gentle with me It felt like I was still dreaming. By the time he had me fully naked, my love box was screaming for him to slide inside. I guess he could tell I was in desperate need of his love making, because he spread my legs and entered me. I gasp out because he was actually bigger than I thought. At first he was going nice and slow, then he sped up his pace. His body was nice

and soft, and he felt good. I knew what I was about to do was wrong, but I couldn't help myself. I closed my eyes, and envisioned it was Brooklyn making love to me. I moaned silently in fear I would call Braxton the wrong name. As he panted and moaned out, I kept my eyes shut the entire ride. He made love to my body for nearly two hours and for the whole course of our sex episode, I kept my eyes closed and fantasized about my husband. Brooklyn.

Chapter 24

Cash Lopez

Cash and Kellz sat in the basement where they would normally sit to watch movies. The two were snuggled up close but neither of them would ever make a move. BJ had been gone to lord knows where, and Breelah was always with Que. Therefore, the two had the chance to bond and catch up on life. Cash had told Kellz about her experience in Cuba, however, she left out the part about Braxton and her six year old daughter. Everyday she thought of her baby girl and this was actually the first time she had been away from her.

Over the last few weeks she had thought about bringing Sky to Miami, but then she thought against it out of embarrassment. She knew sooner or later she would at least have to go visit, but before she did, she had one stop to make.

"You good ma?" Kellz asked looking down at Cash.

"Yes Im fine." she lied. He made her lift up and when she faced him, he knew Cash all too well. Something was bothering her and he hated when she got like that.

Brushing a strand of loose hair from her face, he looked her in the eyes. Though, his thoughts were wrong, he couldn't help himself. She was beautiful. Actually the most beautiful creature on earth.

"Kellz." Cash spoke above a whisper. He was so lost into her beauty, he didn't bother to respond. Instead he kissed her soft lips. When she didn't object, he used both hands to grab her head and went in deeper. He used his tongue to part her lips then kissed her as if it would be their last kiss. So much had went on in their lives, he wasnt sure if it would be their last encounter, and he didn't want to take the chance.

"Crack!" the sound of glass breaking caused Cash and Kellz to stop in there tracks. Cash jumped to her feet followed by Kellz and made their way towards the front of the house. When they reached the living area, BJ was walking back in with the broom and dustpan.

"Boy what yo ass doing?"

"My bad ma, my glass slipped out my hand."

"Boy you drunk."

"No I ain't."

"Nigga I smell it all over you. The shit is seeping out your pores. Move so I could clean this up." Cash said taking the broom from BJ's hand.

As she began sweeping up the glass, she was still slightly embarrassed by the kiss her and Kellz shared. A part of her was glad BJ had came home because there was no telling how far things would have went.

"Where's Liyah ma?" BJ asked hopping she was in her room.

"She on a date." Cash told him with out looking in his direction.

"Fuck you mean she's on a date?"

"Boy watch yo mouth. And like I said she's on a date."

"So you mean to tell me y'all let her go out with some random ass nigga?" BJ looked from his mother to Kellz then back to his mother. Kellz had thrown his hands up in surrender, letting Papi know he had no parts.

"She's not your girl Papi so leave that girl alone."

"Man she gone always be my girl. And ma it ain't yo business. This yo business right here." BJ looked at Kellz with a sly smirk.

"Where yo ass been anyway?" Cash quickly changed subject. There was nothing going on with her and Kellz, so there was no need on having that discussion.

"I was with one of my hoes." BJ said and Cash shot him a *boy you got your nerves* look.

"Ma that's beside the point. You let this girl go on a date with a nigga. When I kill the nigga, his blood on yo hands." BJ stormed off towards his bedroom. Cash sighed out as she shook her head. *This boy was just too damn much.*

"I'm about to head out ma go handle some shit." Kellz said and kissed her on the cheek.

Normally he would stay with her to the wee hours of the night but for some strange reason he had to go. Cash figured it was a woman he was running to but she couldn't be mad.

"Don't look like that Macita. I'll be back aight." Kellz said called her by the funny nickname he had start calling her.

"Okay." she said sadly then wandered off towards the back of the house. Kellz eyes were trained on her as she made her way down the hallway. He too was still caught up over the kiss, which was the reason he was leaving. Once she was out of his eyesight, he shook his head and headed to his car. Cash was heavy on his mind and little did he know, she was also thinking of him.

Laying in bed, Cash had a fountain of tears running down her face. Things were moving so fast and she hadn't even been home a good six months. Right now she was having mixed emotions and the only thing she could do was cry. A part of her was saying *Cash you only live once*, but then their was the guilt. Not only the guilt of Brooklyn, but also the guilt of Braxton back home. She knew Braxton loved her and he was a great father, but, now their faith had been tested. She was beginning to feel as if she was only with Braxton because she had no choice. It was to easy for her not to care. Because he had practically saved her life, she felt obligated to be with him. Kellz, was the typical thug she was used to and the only thing stopping them was, Brooklyn. Had it not been for Brooklyn, Cash would be rolling around her bed with the sexy thug right now as she thought. She missed her some thug lovin and her body was yearning for the thug passion in a real way. Braxton was good in bed, however, he was to gentle with her. She needed to feel the roughness.

The thought of Kellz, had her clenching her legs together. Her love box was throbbing, at just the thought of him. Everything about him was gorgeous. The tattoo of prayer hands on his neck was her favorite. His lips was his sexiest asset, especially with the small moe above his lips. He had perfect white teeth, and he moved like a boss. Kellz was in fact a boss. Him and Nino had made lots of money together, and he even had his own side hustles.

When her phone rang out, she cursed because she was on a nice good ride in fantasyland. The moment she picked it up, a huge grin crept across her face.

Kellz: *I miss you already Macita.*

Looking at Kellz text lowkey made her blush. She chuckled at the name. He called her that because of her inheritance. It was short for mamacita.

Looking at the phone, she didn't know what to say in response but she most definitely wanted to spark up a conversation.

Cash: *Awe, I miss you too.*

Cash: *What are we doing Kellz?*

Kellz: *honestly I don't know. Its something about when I'm around you ma. I know this shit seems wrong but Cash it feel right. Look I don't wanna say to much over this phone but when I see you we will talk about it.*

Cash: *okay. (sad face emoji) so where did you go? Yo little boo called (smirk face emoji)*

Kellz: *Lol awe you jealous?*

Cash: *Noooo (tongue out emoji)*

Kellz: *Whatever. But real shit, I'll never leave you to run to the next bitch. These hoes aint got shit on you ma and don't ever forget that.*

Kellz: *I'll come back if you want me too tho*

Cash: *I would love that. But you good. Ima wait on Liyah then get some sleep. So will I see you tomorrow?*

Kellz: *of course. Don't you see me almost everyday?*

Cash: *Yes.*

Kellz: *Well there you have it.*

Cash and Kellz text for at least another two hours. Just like they did when they were in each other's presence, they were doing the same over text. Flirting, joking and blushing. Cash was actually enjoying the text because she was too shy to say most of the things she wanted to say in person. After this conversation, she knew she would sleep peacefully, however she knew tomorrow she would be totally embarrassed when the two came face to face.

Chapter 25

Kellz

"So who is she?" Adrina asked Kellz the moment he entered the home. She sat with her arms folded over one another on the sofa and her legs shook out of anger.

Every Night Kellz had been coming home late; most nights he wasnt even coming home. Granted Adrina wasnt into the streets, she wasnt dumb either. She knew Kellz all too well which told her it had to be a woman. He was preoccupied constantly, and never paying her any attention. Lately things hadn't been peaches between them, but it had gotten worse, because lately he had been acting single.

Adrina had dealt with so much from Kellz for years. They had been together since high school and throughout the years, she always had to deal with constant bitches. She knew the life he lived came with money and women. However, she didn't care about the money, all she wanted was her family. She had fought women, left him and even threatened to take his kids, and for so long nothing worked. Up until the day of the explosion. She was on her way with Kellz to aboard the second ship, but before they could make it, the water police had the ocean blocked off. Adrian watched in awe, because she had never seen so many police in her life. Kellz who sat quietly, had that gut feeling that it had something to do with his friends wedding. Because of the first wedding, Kellz had a lirey feeling. Flagging down patrol, he was informed of what happened, he instantly went ballistic. Everyday after that day, Adrina worried about him. He would barely eat, barely sleep, he too had lost all his friends on that ship.

After nearly six months, Kellz had finally came around. As time passed, he was doing much better. He had began to run the restaurant Nino had left behind and Adrina didn't have to worry about women. He would come home every night, stopped partying and even wined and dined her. The only thing that mattered to Kellz was his family and finances. Now here they were today, many years later, and something was changing. Kellz was changing drastically and it was breaking Drina down.

"What you talking about Drina?" he spoke breaking Drina from her deep thoughts.

"You haven't been acting like yourself Kelly." she called him by his government name.

"You been staying out, and every time you bring yo ass in this house you smell like another women. I could smell her perfume on you!" she screamed out and began to cry. Kellz stood their unmoved by Drina's tears. He knew that he been acting out differently but he couldn't help himself. This was Cash muthafucking Lopez he was falling for. He didn't mean to hurt his wife, but he too was having mixed emotions over the situation. He saw how things were going with him and Cash, and many times he asked himself *was it all worth losing his family? Hell yes it is*. Was the conclusion he would always come up with.

"I'm around women all day. I have plenty women servers. Hell my whole staff is all women Drina."

"I'm not dumb. I swear when I find out who she is, I'm taking my kids and leaving yo ass."

"Man you ain't going nowhere."

"Try me!" she screamed out with tears rolling down her face uncontrollably. Kellz shook his head and made his way to his bedroom. Because of his guilt, he couldn't stand to look her in the face.

He laid on his bed, and got lost in his thoughts. He reminisced on the kiss him and Cash had shared just a couple hours ago. He thought long, deep and hard about her and he couldn't help but miss her already. He pulled out his phone and began to text her.

Kellz: *I miss you already.*

He waited patiently for her to text back.

Cash: *Awe, I miss you too. Honestly but what are we doing Kellz?*

Kellz: *honestly I don't know. Its something about when I'm around you ma. I know this shit seems wrong but Cash it feel right. Look I don't* *wanna say to much over this phone but when I see you we will talk about it.*

He wanted so bad to tell her how he felt, but he chose to be in her presence when they talked. He wanted to look her in the eyes and pour his heart out to her. He hoped like hell the feelings were mutual between them. A part of him knew Cash was feeling him, but sometimes he was unsure. He knew it had to be about Brooklyn Nino and he couldn't say he didn't blame her.

Cash: *okay. (sad face emoji) so where did you go? Yo little boo called (smirk face emoji)*

She asked making him chuckle. Her ass was jealous which was kind of cute. He had to give it to her though, it was like that woman's intuition had kicked in because out of all the days, she asked that question. True, he did run to a woman, but not just any woman, his wife. He now began to feel like shit because he hadn't told Cash about his family. Right now he prayed she would never ask, because his chances with her would be ruined. He knew Cash all too well, and though she had some player ways, she wasnt one to mess with a married man.

When Adrina walked into the bedroom, she went to her side of the bed and didn't say a word. Kellz lifted off the bed and began to undress. He then laid down and turned his back to her. He picked up his phone and continued to text Cash.

Texting for the last couple hours, everything from her ways to her text was intriguing. He found himself smiling, however, he prayed Drina wouldn't pick up on it. Suddenly, Drina lifted out the bed. Still with his back turned, he paid her no mind. He actually thought she had fallen asleep but her ass was just being nosey. Moments later she crawled back into the bed, and when he felt her naked body cuddle up closely, he became annoyed. He was enjoying his text, and didn't want to be bothered.

"I'm tired Drina." he sighed.

"What you mean you tired? So you too tired to make love to me but you ain't too tired to text."

"Man come on with that shit."

"Come on with that shit? For real Kelly? You know what, fuck you!" she barked then furiously jumped to her feet. She stormed out the room and he could hear the door slam to one if his guest bedrooms. *Good I can call instead of texting.* He thought as he dialed the number.

Moments later, her angelic voice graced the phone. He couldn't contain the smile if he tried too.

"You got tired of texting?" Cash asked and he could hear her smile through the phone.

"Hell yeah. Nigga fingertips numb. All this texting and shit I could have just stayed there." she laughed out shyly. *Damn she even laugh sexy.* He thought. Its crazy how before he always said she was sexy, but because she was off limits, he never paid attention to the little things about her. Like her laugh for instant.

"Yes you should have stayed. Now I'm lonely and shit."

"I told you I'll come back."

"Its almost one in the morning. I'll see you for breakfast right?"

"Yo ass fat ma." they both shared a laugh. "But yeah though, I just wanted to hear your voice and tell you good night." Kellz yawned.

"Okay. well I guess I'll see you tomorrow." Cash stumbled over her words. He couldn't help but laugh because she was too damn gangsta but shy as hell.

"Don't say goodnight, oh, when you know….

"I gotta have your love...Cash finished the song to the Isley Brothers *Don't Say Goodnight*.. They both laughed out. Neither one of them wanting to hang up, they held the phone during a faint pause. Finally Kellz disconnected the line because he didn't want Drina to walk in. He laid back and closed his eyes. He knew he wasnt going to sleep, he just wanted to savor the moment of their conversation. Everything they talked about replayed over and over and when he thought of that kiss they shared, his body became jittery. For the rest of the night he thought about Cash. He never even bothered to go get Drina. She thought she was slick. She always ran to a guest bedroom when she was mad, and Kellz would always wound up in the room with her. But not tonight, this time was different and he was gonna sleep just fine.

Chapter 26

Papi

Papi sat on the sofa in his living room with a bottle of Hennessy clutched tightly in his hand. In his other hand was his 9 millimeter and he wore the meanest scowl on his face. He didn't care how long he had to wait, he wasnt moving until Liyah walked through that door.

When his mother told him she was on a date, his heart sank to the bottom of his Gucci shoes. He knew eventually Liyah would get tired of his shit, but he wasnt mentally prepared for the outcome. To him, he had Liyah in a box. He thought that she would wait for his love forever but he thought wrong. Now here she was on a date. The thoughts of her somewhere giving up what belonged to him, pained him. He told himself over and over he was gonna bust a cap in her but he couldn't shoot his baby, so he was gonna shoot the nigga she was with.

After waiting for Aaliyah to come home, Papi had dozed off right there on the sofa. In his dreams he heard the sound of heels clacking on the marble floors. Realizing it wasnt a dream, he jumped up out his sleep and caught her trying to creep up the stairs. Papi had the house pitch black so she never even saw him lurking.

Click!

The sound of his gun froze Liyah in one spot. Thinking the worst she slowly turned around. She began to panic and her body shook nervously. Suddenly, the smell was all too familiar. His cologne lingered in the air and she knew that fragrance from anywhere.

"Have you lost your mind?" she asked realizing it was BJ.

"I'm the one asking the fucking questions here. Now where yo little date at?"

"He's gone Papi."

"Oh I'm Papi now?" he asked upset. "I'm glad you testing me. You really think this shit a game huh?"

"I'm not your woman. You can't control what I do BJ."

"Yes the fuck I can. You belong to me Liyah. I don't give a fuck what nobody say ma."

"I don't belong to you. You have your bitch and I have my friend." she smirked.

"Oh so you think this shit a joke?"

"Get that fucking gun out my face." Aaliyah cried out. The room was still dark so she didn't know what to expect. She knew BJ wouldn't shoot her but shit he couldn't see and he was crazy as hell.

"BJ what the hell!" the light came on and Cash stood there with her arms folded over one another. She looked at Liyah who looked scared to death. BJ wore a deranged look and right there Cash knew he was in fact crazy.

Liyah looked at BJ and shook her head. She began to walk away, to head to her room, but he called out to her.

"Liyah I'm coming up." he told her then headed past his mother towards the kitchen.

"This child gone be the for real death of me." Cash said then headed back upstairs.

BJ waited for his mother to go to her bedroom before he went upstairs to Liyah's room.

When he pushed the door open, she was naked about to hop in the shower.

"Get yo ass up in here now." he told her seriously.

"What BJ? Why can't you just leave me the fuck alone?"

"I'll never leave you alone. Now lay the fuck down." Liyah looked at him as if he had lost his mind. She knew not to play with him so she layed back on the bed then rubbed her hands down her face. She was growing extremely tired of BJ and his possessive ways. She hated how he did what he wanted to do but tried to regulate her whole life. Some times she actually considered moving out and purchasing a house of her own. It wasnt like she couldn't afford it.

Just like BJ, Liyah was a nineteen year old billionaire. The only thing that kept her around was

Cash because at this point she was beginning to fall out of love with BJ.

When Liyah realized what he was doing, she began to grow upset all over again. *This nigga just smelled my pussy.* She thought in a wow state.

"For real BJ?"

"You damn right. I had to make sure you ain't give that nigga my pussy."

"And what if I have?"

"You ain't dumb ma. That's why you didn't. Now shut the fuck up and let me taste this shit." he told her and spread her legs wide. It had been so long since she felt BJ's touch. Her legs were trembling instantly. His tongue flickered across her clit, and when he stuck his finger in her opening she began to moan out. For BJ to had been so young, and never gone down on a chick but Liyah, he sure knew how to work his tongue.

"This pussy taste good Stinka. Yo can't give my shit away ma." he told her in between licks.

"Ohh Papi." she moaned out. *Oh she wanna play. Calling me Papi and shit. I got something for her ass.* He placed his mouth over her clit and began to make slow circular motions. He could feel her clit harding, and right then knew he had her. After a few moments, she exploded all over his mouth.

"BJ stop please." she cried out. Her clit was so sensitive due to her ogansim, she couldnt take it. BJ lifted from between her legs and peeled out his clothing. Liyah laid back still caught up in the moment, she hadn't realized he was now fully naked. Papi eyed her pussy with so much lust, he was about to pulverise her sweet innocent love box. He had so much built up frustration he needed to relieve. He slid her body closer to the edge forcefully then entered her slowly. Once he worked himself in, it was like he fell into the pit of heaven. Her pussy was nice, warm and tight just how he had left it.

"I love you Liyah. I swear if you ever give my pussy away Ima kill you baby. You hear me?" he asked biting on his bottom lip.

"Yes I hear you. Ohh shit I hear *youuu.*" she was in pure bliss. The feeling was all to good.

He lifted her legs straight up and now had full access to her opening. The nice slow strokes turned into full aggression. He began to beat her pussy up like it was their last encounter. Her moans had turned into weeps and suddenly tears began to fall from her eyes.

"Stop crying Stinka. I love you man." he kissed her tears away without missing a beat of his strokes.

For the next hour they made love, fucked and kissed as if they were still one. Papi hated to see Liyah cry and right now he felt like shit because he knew he was the cause.

After the intense sex, and multiple organsims, they lay there both out of breath. Finally gathering herself, Liyah lifted from the bed and went to take her shower. Papi laid still as if he was sleep, but no matter how hard he tried to block out the sound, it was paining him. Liyah was in the shower and he could hear the faint weeping. He sighed because he already felt bad and she was making matters worse. He didn't mean to hurt her, however, he couldn't get right. He had fell for Monique, he enjoyed the company of Camery but for sure neither of the two could compare to Liyah. He felt like, now Liyah was in his home she was stuck and would always be there when he got there.

After Liyah's shower, she came into the room and laid down besides Papi still wrapped in her towel. He lifted from the bed and went to wash off. He wanted to take a shower but he needed to tend to his baby. After he was done, he walked back into the room. Liyah had her back to him, but he knew she was still awake and more than likely crying. He climbed into her bed and pulled her close to him. He needed her to understand he loved her and soon things would be back to normal.

"I know I hurt you Stinka but I swear I dont be meaning to. A nigga love you to death. Right now its just so much going on around me, I can't even focus. That's why I'm always gone. I can't be here. Everytime I look at you, It hurt a nigga because I know I hurt you. Then when I look at my mom's, that shit hurt me too because I can't rest until I find out what happened on that ship. You, her and Breelah, are the only woman I love on this earth. I'll never give up on y'all. " The more he talked, the more she cried. Finally she turned around to face him and she could see the hurt in his eyes as well.

"Do you still love me BJ? Like really love me?"she asked sadly.

"Hell yeah. Ima die loving you ma. Please don't ever think because we not together right now I don't love you. Don't ever question my love for you."

"So if you love me why are you with her?" she asked referring to Monique. "Is it because she's older? More experienced?"

"At first yeah, I guess you could say that but not in a sense ma. I just got so used to you not being able to come outside and shit. Your grandpa was so strict I couldn't see you when I wanted to. That shit just made me frustrated and basically pushed me into the arms of that bitch."

"Do you love her?" Liyah asked not really wanting to know the answer.

"I fuck with her." he answered nonchalantly.

"That's not answering my question."

"I really don't know. Like I really like the bitch, I guess you could say I love her but not as much as you. I'll never love no bitch as much as you."

"So if you're with her then let me do me BJ. you can't expect to do what you want and I sit back and allow it. Your treating me just like my grandfather. Like I'm a damn prisoner." she cried.

After that statement Papi didn't know how to feel. That shit stuck him like a knife; a sharp knife. He didn't expect her to say those words, even though they were true. At this point, he knew what he had to do; he had to let her do her.

"Just promise me this ma. Promise me you won't fall in love with this nigga." he looked at her with pleading eyes. He couldn't lose his girl to a nigga.

"I can't promise you that." she spoke just above a whisper. A new set of tears came falling from her eyes. After that, there was nothing left to say.

Heart broken, Papi lifted from the bed and slid into his clothing. Once he was completely dressed, he gave Liyah one last look. His heart was crushed and he knew she felt the same way; but the damage was done.

He walked out the room and went into his room that used to be his mother and fathers. After Cash had come back home, he gave her Ms. Lopez's old room and moved into her's which was just as big. He laid on his king size bed and looked up at the picture of his mother and father that hung on his wall. Though he was too young to remember their love war, he knew he was fighting a war of his own. And he would die battling for Liyah's heart.

Chapter 27

Breelah & Que

Breelah and Que had been spending an obscene amount of time with one another, repairing the love they lost many years ago. Finally, making things official, they were both living on cloud nine. Que, who had a whole other life back in Brazil, wasn't fazed one bit by the numerous of text he had been receiving from both women.

Knowing Que all too well, the women knew his disappearance had something to do with a women. However, they would have never thought it was Breelah Carter.

Gabriela, just as well as Keisha, was glad Bree was out of the equation, or so they thought. She was too much of a threat.

Last week Que had purchased a condo for himself and Breelah on Palms Beach. Because the two had spent so many years apart, he felt as if he needed Bree in his arms every night; and this time he wasnt letting her go. Between Que being back and Cash reappearing, Breelah had took some time off from work. She would still help work on a few cases, but she worked from home.

Right now, Que and Breelah laid in their King sized bed still dazed by the sensual sex they had just encountered. Breelah who lay out of breath, had to give it to Que; he still had it. He had fucked her for two straight hours and was ready to go at it again. Kissing the nape of her neck, Que had her giggling like an adorable child. He then slightly lifted up so he could look her in the eyes. *Damn I missed this girl.* Were his thoughts and they were one hundred percent true. Looking into her eyes, was like looking at a pure angel. Just like many years ago, she still held a innocence about her. The only thing changed about her was her now short spiky hair. He loved the look on her. When he first met Breelah, she was fresh out of college and no one around the way had had her. From that day, he had to make her his. Nino couldn't stop him, nor the beef with Carter could stop him. The only person who could have come between the two, was Cash Lopez. However, she was done with Que because of her love affair she had began to have with Nino, so he moved on.

"I love you Bree." Que spoke as he brushed her hair from her face.

"After all this time, you still love me?"

"Hell yeah I thought about you everyday." he spoke sincerely.

"I love you too Quintin."

***Breelah:** I just wanted to tell you I love you and I really miss you. Today's the wedding so I hope and pray I see you there so we could talk.*

Que thought about the text she had sent the day of the explosion. He read the text over and over and even thought about reneging on what he was gonna do. Then came the call from Mario, and he promised him he would handle it. At this point, it was kill or be killed so Que chose the finish the job.

"I have something I want to tell you." Breelah became nervous just thinking about what she was gonna say. Que didnt say a word, but his thoughts began to run wild.

"The day of the explosion I found out I was pregnant. Nobody knew but Brooklyn. To my surprise he wasn't upset." she spoke sadly.

"I'm pregnant!" I blurted out and began to weep.

Brook didn't say anything so I assumed he was stunned. When I looked at him, he wore a confused expression but remained quiet. I didn't mean to say it but Brook and I were so close, I knew he was the only one I could trust with the information. If Carter found out, he would die and take me with him. "Damn, Bree." Brook stood to his feet and rubbed his hands down his face.

"I'm sorry." I cried harder.

Seeing me cry, his face softened and he sat back down next to me.

"There's nothing to be sorry about. Shit happens, ma. Look at my situation, I have two babies that are a few months apart, and them little dudes make life worth living for. It's not a bad thing

and one hunnit, rather Que here or not, you know my nephew or niece gone be straight. I don't know if I ever told you this, Bree, but I'm so proud of you. You didn't follow in the footsteps of me and Carter. I mean, you got yo' head on straight, you smart, you got goals, and more important, you're the best person God has created. In all honesty, a baby is a blessing and you deserve it." He smiled and hugged me.

Just hearing this come from Brook made me light up like a kid at Christmas. Nobody in the world opinion mattered to me like his, and I was now thankful I decided to tell him.

Shocked by what she said about Nino, Que nudged his head back. He knew Nino couldn't stand his guts so he would have expected him to lash out.

"So what happened to the baby?"

"It didn't survive the explosion." Breelah dropped her head.

Que sat there astounded by the information. For the one millionth time, he felt like shit. He murdered his own child.

"I'm sorry." Que spoke candidly.

"Its okay. I mean I never even got a chance to tell you."

Before Que could reply, he received a call from an unknown number. A part of him wanted to ignore the call, but he figured it could be important.

"Hello? " the caller spoke in a rattled tone.

"Yeah who dis?"

"Its me, Arcelie."

Que pulled the phone back and eyed it appalled. *Fuck this bitch want?* He thought to himself. He hadn't smashed Celie in over a year so he knew the call had to be important.

"Whats up?"

"I have something I wanna tell you. Please don't be upset with me, I just feel you have the right to know."

"Im listening."

"Monique's daughter Kamela is yours." she said in a serious tone.

A part of Que wanted to curse her out and tell her she's lying, but another part of him believed it. If anyone knew, it was Celie, because she's the only friend Monique had.

"Man that's bullshit."

"No its really true. I keep telling her to tell you but she's scared. Now that her and Papi are back together, I figured she wasnt gonna say anything."

"Yeah aight good looking." he hung up the phone with out another word.

Breelah was sitting on the side of him with a confused look. He knew she might have heard what was said, however, he prayed she wasnt tripping.

"Did you cheat on me when you made that baby?"

"Nah ma I promise. I had been stopped fucking with her." he lied.

"So what you gonna do?"

"Shit I don't know. What I do know is, she might be mines because all I produce is girls."

"Yo ass just got daughters popping out the woodworks. Damn Que, you gotta start strapping up." she said jokingly.

Though she was trying to act like the information wasnt paining, she was dying inside. Its like everyone gave him a baby but her.

"Damn man. This shit crazy. So Aaliyah mines, Kamela might be mines and Ima have one on the way soon."

"Excuse me?" Breelah neck almost snapped.

"The baby I'm trying to put in you yo." he smirked a sexy smile.

"Boy I'm not having your baby. You got too many babies with bullshit baby mamas. Ugh you got a baby by Hoenique." Bree laughed out.

"Thats fucked up." he shook his head. "But check it ma, how would you feel if they came to live with me?" again Breelah jerked her neck back.

"I don't know about that."

"I just don't wanna seem like I'm a deadbeat. All these years I basically left Liyah for dead. Do you know that was my first time ever seeing her since she was born? And now Kamela mines. Them girls are nineteen plus ma, I gotta at least step up."

"Well I don't mind Liyah. That's my baby. I don't know about that Kamela. And plus her and Liyah can't stand each other."

"Word?"

"Yes Kamela was messing with BJ before her mother. Actually she walked in the room and caught them fucking."

"Ha ha ha. nephew crazy then a mothafucka."

"Yeah, reminds me of someone I know." Breelah rolled her eyes.

Que laughed out because he knew what she was hinting too.

The two continued their conversation, as they lay in one another's arms. Que made a mental note to himself to go holla at Monique tomorrow. For now he was gonna give his baby his undivided attention.

Chapter 28

Monique

Monique rolled out the bed and looked over at Papi who was sound asleep. She wanted so bad to wake him up but she knew he would prolly kick her ass. She was still upset about Camery, and she hated the cold shoulder he was giving her since she had caught him. Everyday after that day, she had called him but he would send her to voicemail. Not being able to contain her feelings, she cried each time. What she didn't understand was how could he do her like that when he was the one who had got caught. Last night he called her drunkenly and told her to open the door. When he walked in, he didn't bother to say two words to her. The mad Papi that she knew all too well, was replaced with a saddened man. Something was on his mind and she could tell it was bothering him.

She watched him as he slept, and he was too damn peaceful for her likings. He was laying on his stomach with his arms folded underneath his head. His locks were pinned up into a bun and he was still wearing his chain. His tattoo of Cash and Nino on his back, looked sexy ass hell, which made her smack her lips. The thought of him entertaining another woman pained her something terribly. Monique asked herself over and over how could she fall for such a young boy, and that's what bothered her so much. As much as she'd seen a future with him, she second guessed herself because she couldn't go through the bullshit he would put her through.

Stirring in his sleep, Papi rolled over and his eyes fluttered open. It was like he could feel someone watching him.

"Man you a fucking creep Smooch." he laughed and turned to his other side.

"Whatever Brooklyn."

"I told you don't call me that." he said not even bothering to look her way.

"We need to talk." she took a seat on the bed.

"About what ma? and why the fuck you up so early."

"I have to go to the salon."

"Aight bye, I'll see you later."

"Papi!"

"I'm just fucking with you." he turned around.

"Look, if its about Camery, she aint nobody. I met her, and just took her out."

"So you never fucked her?"

"No baby I never fucked her. I mean I was gonna try that night but when you caught us, I felt kind of bad." he said as if everything was cool.

"But you telling me I'm yo bitch. How Im yo bitch but you gonna fuck somebody else?"

"I didn't fuck her so it shouldn't matter. Look I didn't mean to hurt you. I swear I'll never do that shit again aight?" Mo nodded her head *yes.*

"Come here baby. Come suck yo dick so you could have a good day at work."

"Boyy!" she hit him with a pillow and lifted from the bed. .

She headed for the shower but she wasn't done with this conversation. She needed to get to the salon for her nine o'clock appointment.

After finding something to wear, she kissed Papi then headed for the shower. She was still kind of upset, but she was glad he had apologized.

When Mo walked into her salon, the place was already packed and she was happy. She needed to busy herself so she could get the thoughts about Papi out her head. That nigga was something else, but he was her baby.

Walking to the waiting area, she called Star, her first client. Star was a top stripper in Miami because she was bad as fuck. Other than her fake ass and fake tits, she still had a pretty face. "Hey Mo." Star greeted her happy to see her girl. The two didn't hang out much but when Mo decided to hit the strippclub scene, she would hook up with Star. "Heyyy Ma." Mo smiled back. The two walked to the wash bowl and began the process. Once they were done, they headed to Mo's chair too began her flat iron. Star unlike most of the girls in Miami had a head full of long hair. Because it was thick and tamed, she never wore weaves.

The moment Star took a seat they began to make small talk.

"Girl I know you gone be fly as fuck for your man Yacht party coming up?" *Yacht party?* Mo thought.

This was her first time hearing about a party Papi was having. The party was actually private but because Papi was thinking about hiring a few strippers Star had found out.

"Girl you know I gotta be the baddest bitch in there." Mo high fived Star.

She was smiling widely, but her insides were boiling. She couldn't believe he had hid the party from her. Normally he would take her to the most high profiled events, so him hiding this made her feel as if he was taking someone else.

Monique flat ironed Star's hair and the entire time she was furious. She hadn't said much since Star mentioning the party, however, she kept mentioning she wasnt feeling good. Mo wanted so badly to call Papi and curse him out, but she had a surprise for his ass. She was gonna show up to the party, dressed to impress and ignore his ass when he tripped over all the niggas that would be in her face.

"His fine balling ass." Star said looking towards the door. Looking over towards the door, Monique couldn't believe her eyes. Que had walked in and was at the receptionist desk. She wanted to run and hide under a rock but it was too late. The receptionist had already pointed to where Monique stood.

"Girl he fine as fuck. I've always had a crush on him." Star jumped around in her seat. Mo was actually shocked by her statement, because Que had smashed everything in Miami. As pretty as Star was, she was surprised he hasn't smashed her.

"Yeah he is fine." Mo tried to play it off.

When he walked over, she studied his facial expression. He looked like a sexier version of Nas but he had deep dimples.

"I need to holla at you." he spoke unmoved by Mo or the cute girl in her chair.

"I'm busy…"

"Man Mo you already know what's up ma. Please don't make me…"

"Give me a second Star." Monique patted her shoulder and walked towards her office.

She knew better than to play with Que. He beat her ass in the past and she was sure he would do it again.

When they walked into Mo's office, she took a seat on her desk and Que sat down on the two seater sofa. Looking around her office, he chuckled to himself. Everything about Mo's office reminded him of Cash's Barber shop. He knew Mo wanted to be like Cash, and now this was all the proof he needed.

"Why you didn't tell me your daughter was mine?" he jumped straight to it.

Mo looked as if she was gonna lie so he stopped her.

"Ain't no need to lie ma. I already know what's up."

"Look Que, I'm sorry. I didn't want to tell you because I knew how you would react. The first thing you would do is call me a hoe and throw a DNA up in my face."

"True. I would have, and I still want one. But that doesn't justify you not telling me. Now you got a nigga out here looking like a fucking dead beat. I already gotta make it up to Liyah and now your daughter. That shit aint cool."

"I'm sorry." was her response and she dropped her head in embarrassment.

"Now I would be wrong if I go upside yo head but I'm not because I've changed. Just give a nigga a test and I won't Kamela to come stay with me if she's mines."

"I don't know about that. I've raised her by myself all these years, so you can't just come into my life demanding shit." Mo stood her ground.

"Its not up for discussion. Handle that and call me when it's time." Que walked out of Mo's office leaving her stuck on stupid.

Seconds later, she was still in a zone. *How the fuck he know? That bitch Arcelie.* She thought furiously. She lifted from her desk ready to give Celie the blues, but she was stopped in her tracks. Papi walked into her office and the look he wore, told her he wasn't too pleased with seeing Que come out her office. *Shit.* she thought as she looked him in the face.

"It's not what you think Papi."

"So what is it then?" Papi crossed his arms over one another waiting for an answer.

Papi had heard all about Monique and Que fucking so right now this wasnt a good look.

"Someone told him Kamela was his daughter." again Mo dropped her head. The silence in the room made her look up and when she did, Papi's look was aghast.

"So how long you been knowing?"

"I wasnt sure when I was pregnant so I never said anything."

"Yeah I bet." Papi shook his head. "Yo you really trifling Hoe'nique." were his last words. He headed out the door and didn't bother to look back. Moniques eyes began to fill up with tears. Its like everything was crumbling around her, and at this point she felt forlorn.

Chapter 29

The Beauty

"Honey what are you in here working on? You've been in here quite a few hours."

"Just give me a minute please Braxton." I wanted to be left alone.

"Are you hungry?"

*"Yes Im starving." I responded eagerly. I had been sitting at this table reading over the paperwork I had finally found. A few days prior, Braxton had come home with a newspaper that blew my mind. It was an article that was over two years ago. When he put it in my hand, my heart dropped. It was a picture of Blaze and Tiny on the front of the cover. The headline read '**Federal authorities make largest drug bust in U.S. history'.** The story also told how the authorities had shot a pregnant Tiny down because she had began to open fire. Soon after, shots were followed by Blaze, who was instantly killed as well.*

As I read, tears began to pour from my eyes like a leaking faucet. I couldn't stop crying as I continued to read. The paper began to tell about the drug bust, the search warrants and even all the properties they had seized. They had seized Tiny and Blazes house, multiple cars, sixty million in cash, four accounts frozen and what took me by surprise was the part about them seizing Trap Gyrl and Club Juice. Blaze's name were on the deeds to my businesses which puzzled me because he had the money to wash every business we had. Right then I knew, it had to be a inside informant. Mike was dead so I was puzzled as to whom.

I continued to read the article and also in bold letters they had made a few arrest. The name that stuck out the most was, Marcus Codly. I clutched my mouth with my hand, and I felt horrible. Marcus was only a computer wiz for my mothers operation. He had no affiliation to our drug empire. At this point I felt like shit. It was good to know he was still alive but that didn't justify the trouble he had endured from our criminal activities. The article stated that they were initially making arrest due to drug trafficking and a numerous amount of murders, and, that's were Blaze name came in multiple times.

Since the day I had woken up from my coma, daily I wrecked my brain trying to remember everyone that was on the ship. Finally after sometime, It came back to me. Tiny, Blaze, Young, Kellz and a few more of Brooklyn and I's friends hadn't made it on the first ship.

"Babe the food is ready. Please come eat." Braxton came back into the room.

"Okay." I sighed and closed the laptop Braxton had purchased for me.

Sitting at the table, I could barely focus. I was so overwhelmed finding out that Blaze and Tiny were shot down. The day it happened, I had a gut feeling that something was wrong. All though I didn't want to believe it, I knew it was something.

"You can't beat yourself up over this Cash. I know it hurts you but you can't go back into that same shell again. Please don't do this to yourself."

"Its just..its..hard for me to accept my friends were killed by the police. Blaze of course he was going out like a gangsta but Tiny did not deserve it. She was innocent in all this."

"Well according to authorities, she fired first honey."

"Yes but there's no telling why. She may have felt threatened. You know there's no telling with them muthafuckas." I pounded my fist into the dinner table.

"She was pregnant." I sobbed uncontrollably. I was distraught
Braxton ran over to my side and began to rub my back. I knew I was stressing this poor man out but shit, nobody asked him to bring me here. He could have left me to die with my friends.

Chapter 30

Cash Lopez

"Cash? Oh, Dios mío" Tiny's mother opened the door in disbelief.

Her wrinkled face and grey hair showed that she was much older, but Cash could tell she still moved around swiftly. She looked over Cash and couldn't believe her eyes. Just looking at Cash, put her on the verge of breaking down. She missed Tiny and her grandkids dearly.

Blaze and Tiny had sent the kids in a limo to the Yacht because they had to bring the firearms for safety. They didnt want Tiny's kids to be in the same vehicle, which is why they were at the Yacht with out their mother.

"Mrs. Vásquez, es bueno verte." Cash stepped into the home with Kellz in tow.

"Hi ju doing Lindo." Mrs. Vasquez referred to Kellz as cute in her broken english. He smiled politely, as he spoke.

"Mrs. Vasquez I can't stay long but I promise to come see you soon. I came by to get the information to where Tiny is buried.

"Oh si mija. I have it right here." she walked into the dining area and opened the drawer to a china cabinet.

Looking around the house, Cash could tell Mrs. Vasquez was living good but she could be better. The guilt from Tiny's death, made Cash want to do something nice for the lady. She made a mental note to write a check before she left.

"Here ju go Mija." she handed Cash an obituary. "You friend come by here too."

"Which friend?" Cash asked.

"yo pienso que fue el bonito con todo los mujeres."

"Que?" Cash asked because she always referred to Que as the cute ladies man.

"Si." Mrs Vasquez nodded.

"que queria el?"

"Don't know Mija but he say he lives in Brazil and be back by to check on me." she began speaking english. *Brazil?* Cash thought puzzled. The fact that Que came to Mrs. Vasquez home, was slightly weird to Cash. however, she brushed it off and prepared to leave.

"Gracias ama." she hugged Mrs. Vasquez long and hard.

Before she walked out, she went into her purse. She quickly signed a check then wrote it out for one hundred grand. Cash knew that Mrs. Vasquez would turn down the money but she wasn't taking no for an answer.

"Imponente mi amor no puedo llevar esto."

"I'm not taking no for an answer. I love you and I'll see you soon." Cash spoke quickly before Mrs. Vasquez gave her back the check.

"Gracias Mija. te veré luego" she kissed Cash checks, smiling widely.

"De nada. te veré luego" Cash walked out with Kellz still in tow. He was smiling widely with the goofiest grin.

"Whaaaa?" Cash blushed.

"I knew you was a gwala ma but damn that shit turned a nigga on. I could tell yo ass don't like talking spanish though."

"Honestly no. I hate it. I use it when I have to."

"Like when a muthafucka talking about you in a grocery store line?"

"Yep. Cash laughed."

"That was real nice of you though ma. That's why I fuck with you. Its like you have a loving heart."

"Yeah I try. I mean, I feel bad about what happened to Tiny. she was so innocent."

"Yeah but you can't blame yourself. Tiny went out like Bonnie because she loved her Clyde." Kellz reasoned.

"True. and that's the part that's crazy."

"And why is that?"

"Because love will make you do some crazy things." Cash looked off into the sky.

"Bae, we gotta get the boat going. The pastor will be there waiting for us."

"But, bae, I don't wanna leave Blaze and Tiny."

"I know, ma. But they slacking and we gotta roll. Have you called them to see where they were at?"

"Yes, four times. Neither one is answering. I hope nothing is wrong." I began to think of the worst.

"Hell nah, ma. Blaze holding twenty-four guns, trust me, that nigga is straight," Brook said and eased my thoughts a bit.

This shit was like Deja Vu.

"I'ma send Kellz and a few more guards to get them, then they gone hop on the speed boat to catch up, ok?"

"Yes," I nodded my head up down.

"Today is your day, ma. After the last time, I don't want shit to ruin this day. Don't stress, baby, they gone be okay, okay?"

"You ready ma." Kellz spoke knocking Cash from her thoughts. She was in a daze as she looked at the tombstones of Blaze, Tiny and her three children she shared with Mike. She looked at Kellz still dazed and with out any words, she shook her head yes.

After leaving the cemetery, Cash's emotions were all over the place. She was thankful for Kellz, because the entire time he held her in his arms. She had left dozens of flowers behind and she promised Tiny and Blaze that she would be back soon.

The drive back home was extremely quiet because Cash was lost in her thoughts. A part of her felt relieved, because she had the closure with her friends that she had been wanting to have for many years.

Suddenly the car came to a stop, and she looked over at Kellz. When he exit the car, she figured he had to use the restroom. Once she saw him lean on the hood, she exit the car and joined him.

Looking into the sky, the clouds were gray and the rain began to poured down intensively. Cash didn't mind because she loved the rain. It was breathtaking and she felt she needed it to wash away her tears. Her long hair became soaked instantly, as she held her head up to the sky. She closed her eyes and took in the serenity. Kellz had walked over to her, but she had no clue because her eyes were closed. He placed a nice gentle kiss on her soft lips then stepped back to let her savor the moment. When she opened her eyes, she licked her lips as if she was trying to taste his kiss. She then grabbed his hands, and pulled him close to her. Right now, she needed to be held and his muscular figure made her feel secure. She then kissed him aggressively which took him by surprise. Loving the taste of her kisses, he opened his mouth and accepted her tongue. The two made out like they were in a movie. In one swift move, Kellz lifted her onto the hood of the car. He then lifted her top over her head and began tracing kisses down her neck to her perfectly round breast. The moan that escaped her lips, turned him on more than he already was.

"Make love to me." she whispered seductively into his ear.

With out hesitation, he unbuckled his jeans then parted her legs. Still kissing her, he used one hand to slide her panties off and wasted no time massaging her womb. He didnt know if it was the rain, or what, but her pussy was dripping wet. He wanted so badly to taste her, but he told himself he would save that for a later date. Right now he needed to feel himself inside her. He used the tip of his head to massage her clit. His dick was so hard it felt as if any minute it would explode. He slid into her tight opening, causing her to gasp out. The inside of her love tunnel was pure bliss. She dug her nails into his back each time he stroked in and out. *Damn did she even get some dick all these years? Her pussy tight like a virgin.* Were his thoughts.

"A nigga love you ma." Kellz spoke enticingly.

"I..I..I love you too." she moaned out loudly.

They were outside in the middle of nowhere. The rain fell down on the two excotical and the only sounds that could be heard were the moans that escaped their lips. It didn't matter who saw them, hell it didn't matter who heard her cry like moans. They were both in heaven and at this point nothing mattered.

"Do you mean it?" Cash asked breaking their kiss.

"Yes ma. I promise I love you." he continued to pound her love box.

True to his word, Kellz had already loved her as Nino's wife, so falling in love with her wasn't hard. Everything about her was impeccable, and now he was really in love because she had the pussy that would make a nigga kill for it.

"Uhhh, I'm about..I'm about too...oh shit!" she screamed not being able to hold it. She had cummed all over his dick and shortly after, he followed.

Chapter 31

Kellz

"Let's get you out this air ma. Yo body freezing cold." Kellz lifted Cash from the car bridal style. He carried Cash to the car and placed her into the leather seats. He went around to his side so he could get inside. He turned on the heater so she could warm up. The rain had began to come down harder, and pretty soon it looked as if it would start hailing. Before he buckled up, he looked over at Cash who was quiet. He hoped like hell she didnt regret what had just transpired.

"You know I meant what I said right?" he asked referring to the *I love you.* It took her a slight minute before she responded and that made him wonder if she did in fact regret it.

"I did too." she turned to look at him. When she grabbed his hand into hers, that made him feel a lot better. He lightly sighed, then started the engine to pull off. But he didn't move. He had a few things he wanted to say, and he prayed she understood where he was coming from.

"I know this shit seem crazy ma, and I don't want you to look at me like some fucked up nigga that just go around smashing my boy's wife." he looked her in the eyes candidly.

"It just feels like, I have to protect you. Everytime we part ways it feels like I'm never gonna see you again. I can't lose you again Cash. I know this sounds crazy but you make me feel close to everyone that died on that ship. Not saying us being together is right, but me being with you makes me feel like that's the only way to protect you. Now, I didnt mean for this shit to happen, but I couldn't help it. A nigga really in love with you which wasn't hard because I already loved you."

"I'm just afraid of what people would think Kelly." she called him by his government name.

"Man fuck what anybody think. These muthafuckas ain't perfect. And this what it is ma." he looked at her one last time before pulling off. He meant what he said and nothing was gonna change the way he felt.

"Just so you know the feelings are mutual. I don't know how or when, but I fell in love with you in such a short time. Its like when I'm with you, I feel secure. Everytime you leave me I be wishing you just come back. I be missing the hell out of you. At first I was sceptical, but it was something about that text the other night that helped me make up my mind. If you're willing, then I'm willing." Cash spoke genuinely.

"And I'm willing." he raised her hand and placed a tenderly kiss on the back of it.

Pulling up to an unknown location, Kellz and Cash quickly got out the car and ran inside. Upon entering, Cash looked around the condo and wondered if this was his home. Apparently he had moved because this wasn't the home he had years ago. Not wanting to pry in his business, she didnt bother to ask. She looked around the home and it was nice and cozy. However, she wondered if he actually lived in there due to the all white furniture that was stain free. Kellz had wandered towards the back of the house and he was back with in seconds. He was carrying an oversized white tee and a pair of socks. He then walked over to a space in the corner, and when he hit the lights, the section lit up red. There was a jacuzzi tub that sat by the picture window. Cash walked over to the area, and was taking back by the view. As Kellz ran the water in the tub, Cash was infatuated with the view. It was a view of the Miami Skyline and the surrounding waters. The buildings were lit up all colors and it gave the sky an exotic look.

"Come on ma, get in so you could warm up. Ima go make you some coco.

"Thanks." she smiled at his gentleness.

Kellz phone began to ring and he pulled it from his pockets. She noticed he had sent the call to voicemail and she figured it was one of his little hoes. Unbothered, she came out her soaked clothing and climbed into the water. Moments later, Kellz came back in holding the cup then placed it on the platform of the jacuzzi. He too began to take off his clothes then gathered his and Cash's and took them to the dryer. Cash watched as he emerged back into the room. This was her first time seeing him naked and boy was it a sight to see. His body was rippled and perfectly sculptured. He was covered in tattoos, and they complimented him perfectly.

When he climbed into the water, Cash pussy began to throb instantly. He was asshole naked but he kept his chain on, which turned her on. Kellz watched Cash hungrily, as her perfect nipples hardened. His dick grew at the sight of her. When she dipped her body into the warm water, he nearly lost it. She came from under the water, hair sleek, and her body glistening. He pulled her close to him and Kissed her forehead genuinely. She wrapped her arms around his neck and they got lost into each other's eyes.

"I love you Cash Lopez."

"I love you too Kelly Camren." she smiled, making him chuckle.

"What you thought I forgot?" she smirked.

"Nah, I know you remember." he said then placed a sensual kiss on her lips. Right then they were so caught up in the moment, nothing mattered, just like the song playing in the background.

These buildings could drift out to sea
Some natural catastrophe
Still there's no place I'd rather be
'Cause nothin' even matters to me

See nothin' even matters
See nothin' even matters to me
Nothin' even matters
Nothin' even matters to me
You're part of my identity
I sometimes have the tendency
To look at you religiously, baby
'Cause nothin' even matters to me

After another round of great steaming sex, Kellz and Cash snuggled in each others arms. Cash had finally dozed off and Kellz watched her as she peacefully slept. His phone rang nonstop and when he checked it, it was Adrina. After she called at least twenty times, she had sent him a text.

The Wife: *after all these years I never thought that someone could come between us. Whoever she is, tell her I salute her because she has you dissing your family for her. I hope you're happy where you are and you could stay there too. I hope she's worth it.*

After reading the text a few more times, he wanted so bad to reply. But fuck that, she nailed it. He changed her name from *The Wife* to *Drina* and he had no regrets. The woman he was with, was worth it and he was happy right where he was at. He kissed the top of Cash's head and she snuggled up closer to him. The way she hung onto him for dear life, made him feel exactly how he had been feeling; like he needed to protect her.

Chapter 32

Aaliyah

"I can't believe your about to do this Venicia." Liyah looked over at her best friend.

"I can't have no baby right now. I'm trying to finish school and shit.

"I feel you but a two day procedure? Its an entire baby in there."

"I know, but I have too. So if you don't wanna take me, I'll just catch an uber." Venicia told Liyah slightly annoyed.

She wasnt really annoyed with her best friend, she was annoyed at the whole situation it self. A part of Venicia wanted to keep the baby and a part of her didnt. She had plans on going to college and a baby would only slow her down.

When they pulled up to the clinic, they watched as all the protesters hung around the entrance door. Venicia looked at Liyah sadly and her heart sank. When Venicia exited the car, Liyah had no choice but to follow. No matter how much she hated what her friend was about do, she had to support her.

Walking into the clinic, Liyah held on to her best friend's shoulder. They walked to the counter and Venicia signed her name on the clipboard. After waiting a few moments, she was called to the back for an ultrasound. Liyah waited out front until she was done. She went to take a seat in the waiting area, and instantly began scrolling thru her phone.

"Where she at Liyah?" Aaliyah looked up at the mention of her name.

Cali stood there with an infuriated glare and he wasn't alone. BJ stood on the side of him with a smirk causing Liyah to roll her eyes.

Every since the night they decided to part ways, they haven't spoken much. Today she was really annoyed because she knew BJ was only there to instigate.

"She in the back." Liyah told Cali.

Without consulting with the front desk, he stormed to the back with Liyah and BJ in tow. Searching each room, he finally found Venicia laying on the bed in a gown. His face showed anger as he stormed into the room.

"Man get the fuck up!" he shouted with veins popping out his neck and forehead.

"Cali? How did you know...?"

"Your mother. Now get the fuck up!"

"No I have to do this."

"Forreal ma? You just gonna kill my seed?" he asked pain in his eyes.

"I can't have a baby right now."

"But Vee that's not your decision to make on your own. Its my baby too."

"I'm sorry Calvin. I can't do this. I'm trying to go to school, I have a career I'm tryna pursue."

"Okay and you could. I'll keep the baby whenever you need me too." he spoke sincerely. "Please don't do this ma." he pleaded.

Venicia began reasoning with herself but she was still unsure. A part of her wanted to back out the moment she heard the baby's heartbeat. It was as if the doctor had done it purposely.

Venicia's eyes focused in on the monitor and seeing the baby's heartbeat on the bottom of the screen made her cry. Cali to watched the screen and he too looked sad.

"You ever kill my seed I'ma kill yo ass." BJ looked over at Liyah. "Get yo ass up girl put some clothes on. I could see that little ass booty peaking out that gown." BJ added then walked out. Liyah lightly chuckled because that boy was a mess. She too walked out the room to give Venicia and Cali some privacy.

The sound of Aaliyah's phone made everyone in the car get silent. Papi who was driving, looked over at Liyah and smirked. Looking down at her phone, it was Cedric, so she let it go to voicemail. Moments later, he called back.

"Answer yo little nigga ma." he spoke with out looking at her. He looked into the rearview mirror and could see Venicia in the backseat chuckling.

"Fuck you laughing at Vee, yo ass back there shook up. Cali got that ass in check." BJ laughed.

“He ain't got shit in check.” Venicia rolled her eyes as if BJ could see her.

“But you still pregnant.” again he smirked. Knowing BJ struck a nerve, no one laughed. Venicia didn't have a come back and BJ left it alone.

“BJ leave her alone!”

“Aint nobody fucking with that girl. That's y'all problem, y'all got some slick ass mouths. But a nigga like me, will put y'all in y'all place. And FYI, don't call me BJ no more, you not my bitch.” he said then turned the music up before she could respond.

Liyah sat on the side ready to smack the shit out of Papi, but she held her composure. She rolled her eyes and turned in her seat. Every now and then, she could feel him watching her so she was about to piss him off. She pulled her cell back out, and began texting Ced. During their conversation, he kept asking why wasn't she answering the phone. She told him that she was in a meeting, so he let up. Their conversation then went on, and he made Liyah smile. Papi picked up on her smile and knew it had to be a nigga. As bad he he wanted to slap her phone out her hand, he had to remind himself Liyah wasn't his anymore. *Is he big mad or little mad?* Were Liyah’s thought as she ignored him and blushed at her and Ceds text.

Chapter 33

The Yacht Party

Cash was in her bedroom looking over her many white outfits. She had a dozen outfits laid out unable to decide which one she wanted to wear. Tonight Papi was taking her out, and for some reason he wanted her to wear all white. She didnt mind because after all these years, it was still her favorite color; other than pink.

Finally deciding on a white dress designed by Sam Edelman, Cash was ready to shut the city down. After her shower, she began dressing. She looked at her long curly hair and suddenly thought of her friend Nikki. Nikki was the only hair dresser in her barbershop and she missed her just as much all her other friends.

Deciding to just wear it curly, she slicked down her baby hair and added conditioner to her curls. Her natural curls hung past her shoulders. Even though her light brown highlights were fading, they still looked good and were now on the tips. Because she had a perfect set of eyebrows, she applied her mac liner, and a coat of glass gloss to her plump lips. She gave herself a once over in the mirror, and was pleased with her entire look.

“Ma you still ain't ready?” Papi burst into the room.

"Yeah I'm just about done."

"You've said that three times." he smirked.

"Boy hush. She playfully hit him with her clutch purse.

"You look nice." Cash complimented her son. He was rocking a pair of white jeans, a white v neck tee underneath a white fur coat. She had to admit, her child had style. With his locks pinned up, his fur and his jewelry, he looked like a rapstar. She couldn't help but laugh when he pulled out his designer shades, compliments of Monique, however, his mother didnt know that.

"Let's roll lady." BJ told his mom then headed out.

When BJ and Cash got to the exterior of their home, Cash was in awe. An Aventador stretch limo awaited them and she had never seen anything like it. BJ helped her in, then climbed in also.

"You ready?" BJ spoke into the phone. When the caller replied, he hung up, then gave the driver instructions to an unknown residence.

Nearly thirty five mins later, they pulled up to a nice residence and pulled over in front of a yellow home. Moments later, Cash noticed a cute, petite girl dressed in a sequin white dress walking towards the car. Papi hopped out to greet her, and now Cash was left puzzled. She wondered was this the chick that had her son occupied. Often, he would stay out all night, even missing days at home.

When the two got into the vehicle, the girl spoke to Cash politely and smiled.

"Hi you doing Mrs. Carter, I'm Camery." Cash smiled at the sound of Mrs. Carter, then introduced herself as Cash.

Cash sat back now again puzzled at the fact that, this was supposed to be her and BJ's time, why would he bring a date? She quickly pulled out her phone and sent Kellz a text because she too was gonna be accompanied by a boo.

Cash: *hey Kelly.*

Kellz: *Lol. sup ma?*

Cash: *wyd?*

Kellz: *in the lab.* Kellz referred to his trap.

Kellz: *why you miss a nigga?*

Cash: *of course I always miss you sexy. Well I was just seeing what was up.* Cash lied. She knew if there was one thing she never did and that was interfere with a man's money.

Kellz: *Ima see you tomorrow because it looks like Ima be here all night.*

Cash: *okay.* Cash text back sadly. She dropped her phone into her clutch then focused her attention out the window. Suddenly she became sadden. She missed Skylar so much she needed to at least hear her voice. Because it was late back in Cuba, she decided to call her tomorrow. She needed to figure something out and fast. She couldn't go on with out her baby girl, but she wasn't ready to face the truth with BJ.

A part of her missed Braxton, but every since she and Kellz been hanging out, she remembered why she loved her a thug. Braxton was a great guy, and true he saved her life, but the truth of the matter is, the heart wants what it wants, and Braxton just did not do it for her. She was only with Braxton because of her good heart. Not to mention, she thought her life in Miami was over. She didnt want to hurt Braxton but she thought pessimistic. Kellz had actually never made things official. All though he told her how he felt, and assured her he was willing, he never asked to take things any further than just a great sex episode.

Every Night Kellz would leave, Cash wondered was he occupying someone else. He was too damn handsome, and had some sex that would turn a nun to a pornstar. Cash in fact wanted to take things to the next level with Kellz, as far as maybe moving in and raising her two children but she would simply wait for Kellz to ask.

"Ma you good?" BJ asked looking at Cash.

"Yeah I'm straight BJ." she half smiled. She didn't want BJ worrying about her, which was something he did constantly, so she chose to always smile when in his presence.

"Where's Kellz? You should tell him slide through." BJ smirked. Cash looked at him and the same smirk followed.

"He's in the lab." Cash repeated what Kellz said, knowing BJ knew exactly what she was talking about. She knew BJ wasn't into drugs, but she also knew he wasnt a dummy; which was just how she wanted him to be raised. Thanks to Pedro he had done a great job. Bj's craziness was inherited, so that she didn't hold Pedro accounted for.

"Well its cool. You don't need him. Ima make sure you enjoy yourself."

"Awe thanks son." she cooed.

Pulling up to their destination, BJ jumped out the limo to help the ladies out. Once they were all out the car, they walked towards the dock where BJ's yacht awaited them. BJ was iffy about the party for a moment because of his mother's past. He wanted her to understand that the past was the past. He knew she loved water, and most of all yachts. He wanted her to forget her past and have the best time of her life; after all, she deserved it.

BJ was no fool, he knew his mother and Kellz were intimate, but he felt she deserved happiness. Now if his pops was alive, shit wouldn't be going as its occurrence, but the fact of his father being gone, he accepted it. He also liked Kellz a lot. Despite him being Nino's friend, Kellz is the one who ran his business, and even stepped up to the role of his uncle and protector. Other than Young, Kellz was the only one he could trust.

"BJ!" Cash called out nervously. Her big beautiful eyes showed melancholy. She was sad, she was worried and she tried hard to hide it, but it showed.

"Ma, its okay." BJ told her to calm her nerves. But what BJ didn't know, was, she was the least bit scared, she just didn't want to revisit that day.

Cash looked at the huge Yacht, and couldn't help but admire it. On the side, was the name Papi and she could tell it costed a grip.

BJ grabbed her hand and led her down the dock. She held her head high, and wanted to make her son happy.

When the three reached the yacht, Cash stood back and smirked at BJ. From where she stood she could see the white and gold balloons and what appeared to be a banner. She walked fully into the yacht, and "Surprise!" everyone screamed out in unison.

Amongst the crowd, Kellz stood front and center with a sexy smirk. Before she could get on his case for lying, everyone pretty much bum rushed her. Breelah, Que, a few staff members from the restaurant, a few of BJ friends and even Mrs. Vasquez was on the yacht. Cash looked around at her peers and smiled widely. The huge banner above said *Welcome Home Cash* and there were tables with plenty of food.

Cash began to mingle into the crowd and of course raid the seafood bar which was her favorite. BJ pulled out his phone and sent a text.

Papi: *aye where you at? You know that surprise I had for you, yeah its here my nigga.*

Young: *Im about ten minutes away*

Papi: *aight*

The DJ began to play Meek Mills hit *Fall Thru* so Papi took Camery's hand and pulled her close to him. This was his song and he was about to get his cupcake on.

You gon' fall through every time a nigga call you
That's why I ball how I ball when I spoil you
We was in Miami, first time I saw you
I was in a Phantom when I pulled up on you
It was late nights, late nights in the bando
Fucking on you good got you bustin' like you Rambo
If you keep it hood so you really understand though
You was there through my ups and downs like a camel

Camery was smiling hard as Papi rapped the lyrics. Looking around the yacht, everyone was in tune with the party. Kellz had hemmed Cash up and everyone on the yacht didn't seem to mind. Shortly after, Kellz and Cash had walked out onto the deck. Papi led Camery over to the table that held one hundred bottles of Ace, and grabbed three. He walked outside to give his mom's and Kellz a bottle but he was stopped in his tracks. Kellz and Cash were in a full fledge tongue wrestling match; Papi couldn't help but smile. He stood back and watched the two as they looked like they were in love. He was happy for his mom because she needed to find happiness again.

Not wanting to interrupt, Papi walked over to the two and broke their passionate kiss.

"Get a room man." Papi said laughing. When they looked over, Cash laughed out embarrassed and Kellz didn't seem to care.

"Here y'all go. And don't get too damn drunk because yall gone fuck around and make a baby." he handed his mother the bottle. Camery stood on the side smiling, she loved how Papi and his mother interacted.

"Good looking Papi." Kellz popped his bottle.

"Dang where's my glass?" Cash asked.

"Ma, you a fucking gee. You don't need no glass. Now Pop that bitch open so we could toast.

Cash, Kellz and Camery all laughed out. Camery wasn't much of a drinker, however, tonight she was gonna indulge. Breelah and Que emerged from the inside, just in time for the toast. Papi lifted his bottle into the air, so everyone followed suit.

"We love you mama, and I'm sure everyone here is happy you're back. Now, I'm not about to get all sentimental and shit, but a nigga happy as fuck to have you in his life again. Oh and this nigga." Papi looked over at Kellz. Cash and Kellz chuckled but Breelah and Que had missed it. "To a new life!" Papi said and everyone clinked their bottles together then took a swig.

"Cash?" a voice said from behind them. When Cash looked over, she couldn't contain the smile that spread across her face. She ran into the arms of Young and began raining kisses all over him. Young, who was still shocked, accepted the kisses astounded. Papi stood on the side smirking and when Young got wind, he ran over to Papi and began playfully punching him. The two play fought for a moment making everyone laugh out.

"Ima kick yo ass Papi." Young was still flabbergasted.

"Look I know you trying to enjoy yourself right now, so Imma let you slide but girl yo ass got a lot of explaining to do Lucy." Young mimicked Ricky Ricardo.

"Welcome home." he extended his arms for another hug.

"What the fuck is she doing here?!" The voice boomed from inside. Everyone looked inside the yachts door. They quickly ran in, and Liyah stood side by side with Cedric. Her arms were folded and she wore the meanest look ever.

For a moment Papi thought she was referring to Camery, but when he looked over he noticed Kamela. *Oh shit.* He thought forgetting about Kamela being Que's daughter. Before he could focus on the matter at hand, his smile was turned into a frown. *This bitch got her nerves bringing this nigga to my mom's party.* He thought looking at Cedric.

"Liyah this your sister." Que stepped up.

"This bitch ain't my sister." Liyah shot.

"Liyah we are sisters, Que is my father too. I'm not with Papi anymore and you aren't either *clearly*. So there's no need for us to be enemies." Kamela spoke shocking everyone.

"Whatever bitch, I ain't got no sisters. So you and your daddy could have a nice life." Liyah shot and walked away. Cedric followed behind her, making Papi follow behind them, but he was quickly snatched up by Cash.

"Not tonight son please." Cash pleaded with BJ.

"Can I just enjoy this night without any drama." Cash asked pensively. Papi nodded his head but still focusing on Liyah and Cedric as they walked over to the Champagne table.

Chapter 34

Still on the Yacht

The light from the moon beamed onto the ocean giving it a exhilarating glow. The slight breeze blew Cash's curls and the stars above had her in a trance. This was the first time she had been on a yacht since the explosion. Braxton had tried to get her on one but each time she declined. Right now she tried her hardest to not think of that day, but it was hard.

Often she would cry because Ms. Lopez had already been taking from her for years and now she was gone again; for good. She missed her mother dearly. Her mind then drifted to Pedro, and he too she missed so much. BJ had told her the entire story of Pedro's death and the part about Pedro wanting his ashes in the ocean to be with his friends; it blew her back. She couldn't help but smile just thinking of Pedro.

"Thank you so much Pedro for raising my child. Even though he's a little crazy, you did an excellent job. I love you and miss you so much." she spoke to Pedro as if he was there.

A lone tear slid down her cheek but she made sure to hold the hundred of tears that wanted to follow.

"Cash, como estas, mi amor?"

"Como estas, Pedro?" I said smiling. He motioned for me to come over. I sat my bag down in the passenger seat and proceeded his way.

"Cash, you have been on the go lately."

"I know, Pedro, it's been so much going on." He looked at me with concern.

"Mi Amor, do you ever think about getting out the game?" That question caught me by surprise.

"Honestly, I do sometimes, Pedro, but it's like the game needs me."

"I understand, I would just hate for something to happen to you. I know you're not a child anymore and Brooklyn will look after you, but this shit is watered down now."

"I understand and soon very soon, I'll be leaving this shit behind me, but right now, I have to keep my mother's business running because no one will run it with respect."

"Yes, now that part I do understand."

I looked at Pedro and he was aging so much. He had gotten old after his family was murdered and I knew because of the tragic death, he didn't want to lose the only thing he had left and that was me.

"So you enjoying yourself?" Young asked bringing Cash from her daze. She turned around and smiled. She was happy to see Young because he was actually one of her workers that she had recruited herself. Taking in his appearance, he looked like he was still getting money, and he had also gotten much bigger. Young was always a skinny guy with a linky frame. Now he had put on some pounds and his hair wasnt in the usual fade, he wore a short fro. Cash had put Young on when he was basically a kid and ever since, he had been solid and loyal as they come. What made her even more happy, was, he was still around to look after BJ.

"Yes this was really nice." she smiled.

"Yeah that boy of yours is something else. I swear he's another *you* all over again."

"You know you're like the tenth person to tell me that." they both laughed.

"Hell yeah. Only thing is, nigga think he could whip some work but his hand ain't fucking with yours." Young laughed not knowing he was actually dry snitching.

"So he's selling dope?" Cash asked looking back out into the ocean.

"Damn you didnt know? my bad."

"Nah its okay Young. Its just, I didn't want that for him. I wanted him to do the opposite of what I did. I can't be mad because he chose to sale drugs on his on...Me." Cash pointed to herself. "I was forced to. My mom was like *fuck college you finna learn how to cook the coke, cut it, then distribute it."* she laughed making Young laugh with her.

"Yeah Ms. Lopez was a beast." he replied and trained his eyes on the currents of the ocean. "I'm just glad you back." Young changed the subject of drugs. "He needed you here. I think the crazy, wild, don't give a fuck ass nigga, came from no adult guidance. Once Pedro died, he was basically left alone out here. Shit he just found me and Breelah about a year ago." Young looked back out into the water. There was a faint pause between the two because they both were lost in their thoughts.

Kellz came from inside of the yacht and walked up on Cash. He wrapped his arms around the small of her waist and Young pretended not to be moved. However, he was very shocked at what he saw, and only wondered how it happened. Young could tell Cash was slightly hesitant, so he walked inside the yacht to give them some privacy.

"You good baby?" Kellz asked because Cash's focus was elsewhere. Right then he figured she was thinking about Nino and a hint of jealousy came rushing through his body. He wasn't mad or anything because he knew how the two were so in love, but he hated when she zoned out because her body language would be distant. He hated when she got like that because she would never open up. Sometimes he would keep prying and when she say *I'm okay, so* he always took it as she missed Nino.

"What are we Kelly?" Cash turned to face him. She wore a melancholy look on her face so that told him she had been giving it some thought. After this conversation, he was gonna take her inside, because he needed her to enjoy her night, instead of stressing.

"What you mean baby?"

"I mean like what are we? We're in love, *so we say.* We don't just fuck, we make love and we spend so much time together. Yet and still you never actually told me you wanted to be with me." Cash spoke looking him directly in the face. She wanted to read him through facial expressions before he spoke.

"To be honest, I don't know ma. Shit in my life is complicated, but like I told you before I'm willing."

"Complicated like what? Do you have someone that you're seeing?" she asked nervously. When he nodded his head yes, her heart sank.

"Its not what you think."

"So what is it?"

"Its really just a complicated situation. But Cash I'm where I wanna be."

"But that's still not telling me anything. You keep hollering this *I'm willing* shit, but that's not telling me shit. Now if you wanna just be fuck buddies, we could be just that." The moment it left her mouth, Kellz became angry. He knew that sarcastic *we could be just that* came from the player in her. Kellz knew all about Ms. Cash and her playaways.

When Nino had first met her, he had told Kellz everything from how they met, up until everything about her and Que's love affair. Cash was a *Mack* at heart, so right now the shit she had just said only made him think the worst.

"Cash you m…." before he could finish, he was cut off by screaming coming from inside the Yacht. They looked at each other and decided to save the conversation for another day. They ran inside to see what all the commotion was about, and suddenly, Cash's heart sank to the bottom of her shoes.

"Monique?" Cash asked surprised by her presence. Monique stood silent, and watched Cash as if she was a ghost. Cash then looked over to a screaming Camery as she tried to run up on Monique. Kellz quickly jumped in and grabbed Camery. BJ ran to Camery's side, and whispered something into her ear.

"You betta control yo old ass girlfriend Papi." Camery shot at BJ causing Cash to be taken aback. Liyah was on the side laughing and Monique shot some slick shit her way.

"Ahh don't be mad at me because yo old ass thought you could tame him. Now look at you, looking stupid as fuck. Keep talking bitch and this be the day I beat yo ass." Liyah shot ready to throw down. She had grown tired of Hoe'nique.

"Wait, BJ you fucking her?" Cash asked with a irate look. *I know damn well this bitch aint fucking my son?* Cash thought walking closer to Monique. She was about to clock her ass but Kellz peeped game and grabbed her.

"Man all these my bitches ma." Papi yelled as if he had enough. He was growing tired all the fussing and yelling at his mother's party so he was about to embarrass them all.

"Yes I'm fucking Monique thot ass ma. I mean it was easy pussy." he spoke to his mother.

"Camery and I just met so she ain't my bitch, yet, but she will be soon. And Liyah while you and yo ol cornball ass nigga over their thinking y'all about to ride off in the sunset, did you tell that nigga who daddy was?" Papi walked over closer to Liyah and Cedric. Cedric wore a shocked look and Liyah drunk ass laughed. In one swift move Papi pulled his gun from his jeans and looked at Liyah in her eyes. All the patrons on the boat, moved towards the door. Everyone knew Papi, and they weren't scared he would shoot the yacht up, but they didn't want to be in harm's way.

"You got five fucking minutes to get this nigga off my shit or he gone be swimming with the fishes literally. And after you take out the trash, take yo ass home and I'll be there to tuck my pussy in." Papi smirked.

Cedric who looked embarrassed quickly walked off the ship, nearly running. Liyah shook her head ready to curse his ass out.

"You know what, fuck you Papi!" Monique shouted on a verge of crying. Right now she was not only embarrassed but she was also scared to death. She knew by the way Cash was looking at her, that shit was about to escalade. She used being mad at Papi, as her excuse to storm off.

"Camery, I apologize about all this shit ma and Ima see you soon. Now I know you might not wanna fuck with me after all this but a nigga do wanna fuck with you. As of now I'm single as muthafucka so if you ain't tripping bang my line. Ima have one of my drivers drop you off to the crib so you could head outside." Papi told Camery then kissed her on the forehead to assure what he said was real.

Papi was so caught up in the moment, he nearly forgot he had his gun still out. Little did he know, he had turned not only Camery *on* but Liyah *on* as well.

"I'll hit you tomorrow." Camery blushed. Before she walked away, she shot Liyah a smirk then headed out into the night. Staying true to her word, she was indeed going to call Papi. she wasn't mad at him at all, in fact she loved the way he moved and most of all, she loved his realness. Liyah who was ready to pop off, left it alone remembering it was Cashs' party, however, she had something for her just as well as *Hoenique*.

The night was winding down, and now it was just Liyah, Kellz, Cash and Papi. after all the mayhem, everyone had left. Papi could tell Cash was upset about Monique, but she was also acting weird towards Kellz. He brushed it off as their business, because he had enough of his own shit going on.

"Let's go ma." he looked at Cash. "and bring yo ass on too." he told Liyah then headed out the door. Once they were in the limo, Papi looked out the window and peeped Kellz looking like a lost puppy.

He wanted to get out and holler at him but his moms was mad so he wanted to get her away from him.

"Ma you had fun?"

"Despite all the bullshit, I sure did." Cash beamed.

"That's all that matters." he smiled then focused his attention out the window. So much was going on with his love life, the shit made him just want to be fully single. He was in love with Liyah, he loved Monique and he was now starting to like Camery. After seeing Liyah on the arms of another nigga, Papi knew sooner or later he had to make up his mind. It was either be a player, or get his girl back. Being a player was a hard pill to swallow because he knew there would be drama.

He looked over at Liyah who was quiet as she stared out the window. *I don't know why I be doing this shit. She pretty, got good pussy, aint no thot like the rest of these bitches and she love a nigga to death.* Were his thoughts before laying his head back to zone out. He was gonna get his shit together, but he needed time. Granted he was a player, he knew deep down, Liyah was gonna be the one he married and dropped a couple babies in. Right now she was trying to play the game with him. He knew it wasn't her, so, soon, he was gonna be the prince Liyah awaited.

Chapter 35

Que

a couple weeks later….

Que pulled up to Cash's home and dead his engine. He sighed lightly because this shit was about to be hard. However, he prayed his plan would work because he needed his girls to get along. Over the course of time, Que had already felt bad about abandoning Liyah, and now he felt like shit about Kamela. Everyday since finding out Kamela was his, he had been trying to step up to the plate. When he asked her if she wanted to stay with him, she was extremely happy. From what she had told him, she couldn't stand her mother. She also told him about Papi being hers and even catching them fucking. Que couldn't do shit but laugh. He kept his thoughts to himself, but he was happy to know she understood why he wasn't in her life.

"So do you think she's gonna come?" Kamela asked unbuckling her seat belt.

"I don't know. She might." Que said then opened his door and hopped out.

The two walked up the driveway that led to Cash's home, and rang the doorbell. Cash came to the door wrapped in a towel with a two piece on.

Que couldn't help but admire her because she was still as sexy as the last time he had seen her.

"Hey." Cash politely spoke to Que and Kamlea. She opened the door to invite them in, then locked it behind them.

"Cash whats up? Is Liyah here?"

"Yeah she's up in her room. She's not feeling well."

"Okay can you call her down here?"

"Sure." Cash said then walked over to the intercom.

About ten minutes later, Liyah came down also wearing a two piece. Her and Cash were about to go for a swim. *Her ass ain't sick.* Que thought eyeing her as she came down the spiral stairs. When she got to the bottom of the stairs, she stopped. She shot Que a *what you won't* look, then looked over at Kamela with a frown.

"Liyah look ma. Whether you like it or not, y'all sisters. Now I don't know what y'all little beef about, but that shit needs to stop. Y'all both my daughters, and I want to spend more time with y'all. Kamela already decided to come stay with me, so you need to pack your stuff and come too."

"I'm not moving with you!" Liyah crossed her arms over one another.

"Just give up she aint…" Kamela was cut off.

"Cash please don't make me go. I want to stay here with you." she whined on a verge of crying.

"Of course you could stay with me. Your nineteen now, you basically make your own decisions." Cash told Liyah. Liyah snuggled up under Cash's arm like a seven year old child. She was where she wanted to be and that was with Cash.

"Just at least give it some thought Liyah." Que spoke despairing. He really wanted this for his girls, and Liyah had just ruined his moment. He shot Liyah one last look, but when she turned her head, he chose to just leave.

Que and Kamela headed out the door. He knew Liyah loved Cash but he also hoped she would at least give it some thought. Looking at his ringing phone, Que really didn't feel like being bothered. He looked at the caller ID and sighed out, before answering.

"Yo?"

"So you choosing this bitch over your family?" Keisha spoke into the phone angry.

"Fuck is you talking about?"

"I'm talking about this bitch that suppose to be dead. She popped up in my explore page and what do I see? You laying in the background in some fucking draws. Then the fucking caption was *his old flame is his new wife*. What the fuck does that mean?"

"I don't know shit."

"So you got us all the way out here while you starting another life with this bitch in Miami? You got shit fucked up Que!" Keisha screamed before slamming down the phone.

"So how is Breelah gonna feel about me living with you guys?" Kamela asked the moment Que was off the phone.

"Shit she really don't have a choice. A nigga been away from y'all for all these years, I gotta step up to the plate." Que looked over at Kamela. It was crazy because she actually looked just like him. Kamela and Liyah favored but Kamela and Qui looked identical. Because Liyah was mixed, she had a lighter skin complexion and long natural hair. Kamela on the other hand, had the same skin tone, and wasnt breeded with shit but full blown nigga.

The car had become silent, because Que was caught over Liyah not wanting to live with him. He wondered if she knew Cash was the one that killed her mother? He thought about exposing the information, but then thought against it. He didn't want to turn Liyah against Cash so for now, he would let her be.

After dropping Kamela off to his condo he shared with Bree, he told the ladies he had some shit to handle and he would be back with food.

Forty minutes later, he pulled up to his destination and hoped like hell this shit wouldn't backfire on him. Knocking on the door, he waited for her to answer. When she opened the door, a sexy grin was plastered across her face.

"Sup Mo?"

"Hey Que." she smiled and invited him in. because he knew Kamela was gone, he walked straight to Mo's bedroom and took off every piece of clothing. Little did Mo know, he was actually being petty.

Chapter 36

Papi

Pulling up to his trap, Papi couldn't wait to cook his work and go home. For some strange reason, he was always tired. Right now he just wanted to shower and get in his bed. Every since the yacht party, Monique had been blowing up his phone and that shit was starting to annoy him. Most of the time he was in the company of Camery, so he would send her to voicemail. Over the last few weeks, him and Camery had been getting pretty close. He enjoyed her company and now he enjoyed her sex. Two days after the party, she had invited him over. When he arrived, she was wearing a come fuck me dress with her ass nearly spilling from the bottom. When he walked in, she had candles lit and a bottle of Ace sitting inside a bucket of ice. He wasted no time opening the champagne, and also helping her out of the dress. Every since that night, Camery and Papi had been fucking nearly everyday. And that was another thing he blamed his tiredness on. Since he and Camery had been kicking it tough, he barely got any sleep. They would stay up all night, drink and have wild sex. It was like he was turning her out, but it was for the better. Her drinking made her loosen up more than she already was. Her ass turned into a straight freak, and that shit drove him wild. He fucked with Camery the long way and enjoyed everyday spent with her.

Not even five minutes after walking through the door, Papi cursed himself for not looking closing the wood door behind himself. Monique was at the door and she used her hands to look thru the bar door. She saw Papi standing in the kitchen, and he knew he was caught.

Walking over to unlock the door, he walked back into the kitchen. He pulled out the pyrex jar, baking soda and a huge pot. Monique took a seat at the table but didnt say a word. Papi moved around the kitchen as if she wasnt there. She was the one invaded on him, so she needed to be the one that spoke first.

"So its like that?" Mo asked getting annoyed.

"You tell me Mo."

"How can you be mad about something that happened before you?"

"It happened before me but you still aint tell me."

"I wasn't too sure."

"Damn you smashed that many niggas?"

"No." Mo quickly answered.

"Man what you want from me Mo? You see the way I move but yet and still you chose to stick around."

"So why would you tell me we are together? Why didn't you just do you and let me do me?"

"Because I don't share my pussy. If its mines then its mines."

"But I gotta share your dick? Like forreal Papi? You fucked me, my daughter and her sister"

"Damn I never thought of that." Papi laughed. When he saw the serious face Mo shot, he got serious.

"I haven't fucked nobody since I told you we were together. I wasn't even fucking the bitch I'm in love with." Papi looked up from the pot.

"Oh so you in love with her?"

"Hell yeah I'm in love with her. When all you hoes gone, Liyah gone still be here. You or nobody else could come between that."

"So did you smash that other girl?" Mo asked quickly changing the subject.

"Yeah I fucked her. Pussy good too." Papi smirked.

"I'm not laughing Papi Im dead ass right now."

"I am too. Her pussy fire as fuck."

"Papi!"

"Man quit getting all butt hurt. I didn't fuck her until after the party. But does it matter? Me and you ain't together."

"So that's just it? We over?" Mo asked on the verge of crying. She knew how to get to Papi but little did she know those tears wasn't working today.

"You really want me to answer that?" he looked over.

"Please just give me a chance to make shit better. I'm sorry about the situation with Que but I don't want to lose you."

"So you gone let me do me and you do me?" he smirked again.

"So you want to fuck other bitches but I can't do shit?"

"Exactly what I'm saying." he focused back on his work.

"Whatever Papi."

"So is that a yes?"

"I guess man." she spoke unsurely. Papi looked over to her and couldn't believe his ears. She thought she was doing something by accepting him to do as he pleased, but little did she know he was now turned off. Any bitch that claimed they loved someone, would fight for their love. Monique now looked weak to Papi and after today he would treat her like the hoe she was.

"Why you didn't tell me your mother was alive?" Mo now looked worried.

"Because that wasn't yo business. Just like it wasnt yo business to pop up to the party. That party was for my mom while you think a nigga tryna be sneaky and shit."

"My Bad. I had heard about it from a friend."

The sound of someone knocking on Papi's door, astounded him. No one knew where this house was except, Monique and Young. The only reason Mo knew was because she sometimes helped him weigh and sack up his work. Papi wiped his hands off, and walked towards the door. When he looked out, his head tilted back and he cursed himself silently. He couldn't hide because his car was outside. Also he couldn't just leave her standing there because anything could happen. He unlocked the door nervously then headed back into the kitchen.

"Yeah you think I didn't know where yo little ass was at."

"What you want lady?" he nervously laughed.

"You know what I want. To see what yo ass up too." she walked into the kitchen. When her and Mo locked eyes, Cash shifted her weight to one leg and pursed her lips. She watched Mo through an enraged pair of eyes. Mo began to fidget in her seat as she dropped her head. She looked nervous and was ready to leave right this moment.

"Well hello Monique."

"Hey Cash." Mo smiled nervously. Papi walked back over to the stove and he too was nervous as hell.

"Bitch don't hey Cash me. See I wouldn't be tripping had I come back and you were still around. That was years ago and I'm trying to put my past behind me. But tell me this, out of all the niggas in Miami why my son? Or is because you smashed them all and BJ was the only thing left?"

"No..I...Me..I didnt know he was your son until after we had sex. I swear I didn't know."

"Well I'm sure he told you his age and you still decided to fuck on him. What could yo old ass do with my fucking son that he can't do for himself?"

"Well I have a business now and he's the only guy I fuck with. I swear Cash I genuinely love him." Mo burst out into tears. Cash looked over at BJ who seemed to not be paying attention. Or at least he acted as if he wasn't.

"Ha! Since when were you ever so faithful? And love?" Cash laughed.

"Papi you love this bitch?" Cash turned to her son.

"I did ma. Damn stall her out."

"Give me one reason why I should stall her out?"

"Because I don't be in your business that's why." Papi smirked knowing she knew exactly what he was talking about. Cash side eyed Mo, then looked to her son.

"Yeah okay and when this bitch fuck over you, don't say I didn't warn yo ass."

"Um...Ima go." Mo stood to her feet. She looked at Papi to see if he would at least walk her to the door but he didn't budge. She looked at Cash one last time then walked out without another word. Cash lifted from her seat to lock the door then came back to badger Papi.

"You really love her?' Cash asked surprised.

"I ain't gonna lie, I did for a minute until all the bitch skeletons started coming out to play. Monique cool as fuck ma her past just fucks it for her."

"Yeah that one right there ain't no joke. She done ran thru the whole Miami BJ. and the bitch a sack chaser. I just don't want you getting caught up with someone like her."

"I'm good ma trust me." Papi assured her. Cash left the situation alone then headed over to the stove where he stood.

"Boy give me this. Let me show you how to whip some work." Cash snatched the spoon from Papi. He couldn't help but laugh because, as boojie as she acted now, her ass was still hood and a real life *Trap Gyrl.*

Chapter 37

Cash Lopez

"Man we need to talk." Kellz rushed into the house. Cash folded her arms unmoved by his presence. After the night of her party, she had been avoiding him. The few times he had come around her, she acted nonchalant. Their conversations were now dry and even their text had eased up. Each time, Kellz acted unbothered by her attitude. He was still going on day for day as if everything was okay. Meanwhile, Cash was bitter and slightly broken. She knew she couldn't be mad at him, which she wasn't. She was actually hurt. Kellz never told her who the woman was, but for him to finally admit, she knew he really liked her; if not in loved her.

Cash walked down the hall to the spiral stairs that led to her bedroom. Kellz was close behind anticipating this talk they were about to have. When they made it to her bedroom, Cash began to search her closet for an outfit. Tonight she had plans on going to BJ's club because she had grown tired of sitting in the house.

"Where you going?" Kellz asked watching her fumble thru her clothing.

"BJ's club." she responded dryly just as she had been doing lately.

"Damn I thought I could come talk to you then we could chill. Maybe order some food and have a drink."

"Well I don't want to sit in this house. I wanna go out, get drunk and shake my ass." she said to piss Kellz off. Kellz laughed it off, because he knew if Papi was there, the shit wouldn't be going down.

"Well I'm going with you so I could let some random bitch shake her ass on me." Kellz smirked.

"Fine with me." she shot over her shoulder. Kellz lifted from the bed and walked over to the closet. He snatched her up off her feet and walked her over to the bed.

"Put me down!" she shouted pretending she didn't want to be in his arms.

"Man yo ass ain't going nowhere." he snatched the dress out her hand she was still holding on to. "You about to sit yo ass right here and holla at a nigga."

"Holla about what? There's nothing to talk about Kelly. You in love with the next bitch, I'm just a fuck buddy and that's what it is."

"Man you ain't just my fuck buddy. Stop saying that shit!"

"Well what is it then? Because yo ass sure been avoiding this conversation."

"I haven't been avoiding shit. You just throwing yo little tantrums and shit ma."

"So what does that tell you?"

"Honestly? that you need your space."

"You just don't get it." Cash shook her head and stood up.

"I do get it, and thats why Im here. Cash you my bitch ma. Excuse my french but you are. I'm with you everyday and I love the time we spend together. When you came back, a nigga had a whole ass life going on. I didn't expect to fall in love with you. So this shit is hard for me."

"I understand that. And I didn't mean to complicate things in your life. Whoever she is, just be with her." Cash walked back over to her closet. She was ready to just give up on everything.

"You not complicating shit. Just give me some time to figure shit out. I swear its gonna be us ma." he spoke sincerely.

After that *give me some time* speech, Kellz basically blew it. Cash wasn't the type of chick to be put on a back burner. She knew her worth and she wasn't short changing herself for no nigga.

"Man come here ma." Kellz pulled her close to him. She was so beautiful when she pouted.

"No, I ain't fucking with you." Cash blushed.

"You gone always fuck with me." he spoke looking directly into her eyes. She tried her hardest to hold her smile. *This nigga fine as a mouthafucka. Why he had to come over here? Shit.* She thought as she blushed. He playfully pulled her on top of him and now they were face to face.

"Cash I really do love you." Kellz spoke genuinely. He really loved Cash, however he had to figure things out with Drina.

"I love this dick, ohhh I love this…." Cash whimpered as Kellz took her body to ecstasy.

"I love this pussy ma." he spoke as he hit her with nice and slow strokes. The sweat between the two, dripped off their bodies onto the silk sheets. Cash was doing everything from moaning to calling out Kellz name.

"You missed me baby?" he asked her because of their awkwardly separation.

"Yesss...ahhh...yesss I missed you." Cash cried out. Kellz was hitting her spot, and this was exactly what she needed. He bent down to give her a kiss and she accepted aggressively. After the heated kiss, Kellz instructed her to lay flat on her stomach. He wasted no time sliding back inside of her.

"Shitttt." he howled out. Her pussy was so tight and it was gripping his dick like a glove. Because he didn't know about Braxton, he wondered if she had actually been saving herself. Her pussy was too tight to have been tampered with.

Lifting her ass cheeks, he made sure to slide every last inch inside of her. She moaned loudly until he was fully inside. Once he was all the way in, she began to fuck him from the bottom. Twirling her pussy from underneath him, she could feel the pulse in his dick began to thump and it only meant one thing, he was about to explode.

"Cumm with me baby." he told her on the verge,

"Right there. Oh my god right there and Ima..Ima...ohhhh shit bae!" she cried out loudly.

They had cum together, and now they both were breathless.

After regaining her composure, Cash lifted out the bed.

"Where you going ma?"

"I'm still going clubbing." she joked.

"Yeah okay get that ass beat." he laughed still out of breath.

Seconds later she came back into the room. When she grabbed her robe he knew where she was going. Kellz lifted out of bed, and joined her in the shower.

When he stepped in, he rained kisses all over her neck. Her body was soft, and blemish free, except for the burn from the explosion on her back. The mark had faded away but it was still noticeable.

She turned around to face him and for some reason she looked hurt. He looked into her eyes, not to read her but to assure her, he was right there, and never going anywhere.

"When you told me you would do anything to protect me is when I fell completely in love with you. I just hope you protect my heart because that's a part of protecting me as well Kelly. I've been down that road, and I don't wanna go back." Cash told him apprehensively.

"When I said I'll protect you, I meant it Macita. I'll never hurt you." he watched her eyes as they spoke volumes. He kissed her passionately. Cash wrapped her arms around his waist, and laid her head on his chest. She closed her eyes and for the first time, she had a clear head; And this is where she wanted to be.

Chapter 38

Kellz

The next day, Cash and Kellz woke up in each other's arms. They had spent their entire night talking, drinking and cuddling. Cash, who was now cooking breakfast, waited for Kellz to meet her in the kitchen. Kellz lifted out the bed and the first thing he did was check his phone. He had many text and calls from Drina as usual. He ignored her calls then headed to the restroom to handle his hygiene. After he was done, he slid into his bball shorts he had over Cash's house. He headed downstairs. On his way, he bumped into Liyah who looked as if she had been up all night.

"You good Liy Liy?"" Kellz asked her worried.

"No uncle Kelly. I can't stop throwing up." she clutched her stomach on the verge of crying.

"Okay Ima send someone to get you some stuff." Kellz told her referring to the staff outside. There were plenty guards, pool service and many others that were always outside the home. The only thing they didn't have was a cook because Cash had fired them. She said she wanted to be the one to wait on her son hand and foot, but Kellz knew better. That was the one thing that told him she had a man back home, because she was doing things that only a wife would do. Cash was royalty, so her cooking and cleaning was a surprise.

"Thank you." Liyah dragged into her bedroom.

Kellz headed downstairs and went to the kitchen. When he walked in, Cash was over the stove whipping up some bacon, eggs, potatoes, grands biscuits and hash browns. He kissed her on the neck then snatched a piece of bacon off the tinfoil pan.

"Babe call John."

"Why whats wrong?"

"Its Liyah. She sick as fuck. She looks horrible. We need to get her some meds"

"I know. She's been looking like that for about two weeks. Everything I give her she won't hold down. I think she has the flu."

"Nah ma. Her ass pregnant."

"Damn I didnt think of that." Cash stopped cooking. The thought of her being a grandma, crossed her mind. She knew it wasnt Cedric's because she rarely dealt with him.

"Hell yeah. Papi done made you a granny." Kellz laughed wrapping his arms around Cash.

Shortly after, Cash went to the intercom and buzzed John. She told him to send someone to the store, then rattled off the things she needed. She then went to the cabinet and pulled out a can of Campbell soup and crackers.

After making her and Kellz a plate, she spooned the soup from the pot into a bowl, and took it upstairs to Liyah. When she came back down, she sat at the table with Kellz and began to eat. Cash and Kellz talked about everything under the sun. No matter how much the two conversed, it was like they had just met.

By the time they were done, Cash was ready for her daily swim. Normally, Kellz would have left to get his day started, but for some reason he didn't want to leave Cash's side. The guilt of Drina, weighed heavy on his mind, and after last night, he had a lot of proving to do.

Cash went upstairs to slide into her bikini. When she finally came down, Liyah was with her and she looked much better. Kellz made a mental note to holla at Cash about getting her to a doctor. But for now he would let up so they could enjoy their sunday afternoon.

Kellz watched as Cash and Liyah raced back and forth across the pool. He couldn't help but laugh because Cash had this swim shit on lock. She had beat Liyah twice and was happy as if she won the nobel peace prize. Cash came out the pool to take a sip of her Cadillac Margarita, that Kellz had whipped up. When she walked over, she was smiling from ear to ear.

"Can't nobody fuck with me." she boosted.

"Girl Ill out swim that ass. Kellz said laughing. He stood to his feet, and quickly dived into the pool. Cash followed and dived in.

"Get him mommy!" Liyah screamed laughing.

Kellz and Cash were at the end of the pool.

"1...2...3!" Liyah called out and they took off.

By the time they had made it to the other side, Cash had touched the pavement, and Kellz was still in the middle of the pool breathing as if he had ran a marathon. Cash and Liyah were both laughing. Cash got out of the pool to take another drink and she noticed the buzzard ringing. She answered it knowing it was the front gate security.

"Hey."

"Mrs. Carter, you have a guest here by the name of Adrina Camren."

"Who?" Cash asked puzzled.

"I don't know, she says she's here to see Kelly."

"Okay let her back." Cash sat the buzzard down and began to dry her hair.

From across the yard, Kellz watched her in her two piece and admired every curve. He then hopped out the pool, followed by Liyah and they made their way over to the chairs.

"Yall can't fuck with me." Cash taunted both Kellz and Liyah. Kellz pulled her into his lap and playfully punched her in the ribs. She laughed out hysterically as Liyah laughed on the sideline.

Moments later, Drina walked through the gates. When she saw Cash, she stopped in her tracks because she couldn't believe her eyes. *This bitch suppose to be dead.* She thought as she watched the two play fighting. Drina knew Cash was once married to Nino, but right now, she was a bit confused. She was in Kellz's lap, laughing as if she didn't have a care in the world. Kellz hadn't noticed her, and he too looked mighty comfortable.

"Cash?" Drina asked slightly confused by her presence. Cash looked over at the woman and had the slightest idea of who she was. Because Cash had only met her twice in passing, she was puzzled as to who the woman was. But all that came to a halt because of the facial expression that Kellz wore.

"I'm sorry but who are you?" Cash asked.

"Im Adrina. Kellz's wife." she stated.

"Kellz? Wife?" Cash looked over at Kellz.

"Man what the fuck you doing here?" Kellz asked astounded.

"Find my iphone." Drina smirked holding up her Iphone 7.

"Okay but what do you want?" Cash stood from her seat still drying her hair. Kellz quickly jumped up because he knew what Cash was capable of. Apparently Drina didn't know because if she had, she would have never made the mistake by coming.

"So this is where you've been?" Drina asked.

"Yes this where he's been. And this is where he will remain." Cash protested.

"Is that true Kelly?" Drina challenged.

"Man go home Drina." Kellz added. He was frustrated with her being here.

"Go home? Wait are you guys seeing each other?"

"Yes we are." Cash interrupted.

"So this is what you're doing? Sleeping with your dead friend's wife."

"All that don't matter. Just no this where he wants to be."

"So is that true?" Drina focused her attention to Kellz. Tears began to pour from her eyes and her lips began to tremble.

"You're gonna just throw everything away? Our marriage, our family, everything we've invested." Drina cried out, making him feel like shit. "Answer me Kelly!"

"Yeah answer her Kelly." Cash added. She was growing impatient. She was waiting for Kelly to chose his wife so she could go on with her life.

"Man this where I'm at right?" Kellz looked from Cash to Drina.

"Just come get yo shit!" Drina spat furiously.

"Man you could have that shit. I'll be there to get my bread and jewelry."

Without another word, Drina stormed off with a brand new set of tears. She was beyond hurt.

Cash headed inside the house. She was upset that Kellz didn't tell her he was actually married. However, she couldn't believe that he had chosen her. She walked to the bar to pour herself another drink. Right now she didnt know how to feel. Kellz had went upstairs and laid across Cash's bed. He couldn't believe Drina had actually showed up. The tears in her eyes had Kellz feeling horrible but he couldn't help how he felt. He knew with Cash he wasn't making a mistake. He didn't mean to hurt his wife, and yes he loved his kids, but like he always said, he was where he wanted to be.

“So why you didn't just tell me you were married?” Cash asked walking into the room.

“You would’ve stayed with me knowing I'm married?” he asked. Cash was taken aback by the question and truly didn't know how to answer.

“Exactly.” Kellz said in a *of course not tone*.

“So what made you choose me? I mean I know y'all have history and I just came back around.”

“Real shit Cash, you not the type of bitch a nigga could just put on the back burner. I couldn't take the chance of missing out on the opportunity of having you. True I feel fucked up, but something in my heart telling me I made the right choice.”

“So I guess this means were official?” Cash asked unsurely.

“We been official baby.” Kellz pulled Cash into his arms. She kissed him proudly, and he accepted. He grabbed her face, and placed four more kisses on her forehead down to her lips. He knew he had made the right choice, and he was never gonna let her go.

For the remainder of the day, Cash and Kellz laid up and watched movies. It was a sunday, so the day was pretty relaxing. Later Cash would go hook up her sunday dinner, and the two would spend time as a new couple. Just that fast, things felt different.

Kellz was happy, Cash was happy and nothing could steal their joy; or at least for now.

Chapter 39

Aaliyah

"So what does it say?" Cash asked Liyah eagerly. Liyah didn't respond but the look on her face told Cash exactly what she knew.

"Why so sad?"

"Well I didnt quite expect my first child to be by a guy who I'm not with. I mean I know he might be happy but it wasn't my initial plan. I wanted to raise a child in a two parent home. Something I didn't have." Liyah spoke with glossy eyes.

"I understand. But give him some time baby. I'm sure he'll come around."

"Same thing he keeps saying." Liyah looked sad. "Can we keep this between us for now. At least until I figure out what I'm gonna do."

"Yes. but I hope you're not contemplating an abortion."

"Nah. that's not it." Liyah assured Cash. as bad as she wanted to have an abortion, she thought about the day Cali and BJ had came to the clinic. At the same time, she didnt want to seem like a hypocrite because she begged Venicia to keep her baby.

After talking to Cash, Liyah headed up to her room. Cedric had called her on the way up but she didn't bother to answer. She had so much on her mind she couldn't focus on Ced. After the party, she was actually shocked he was still interested but little did he know, Liyah was now turned off. She needed a man that would stand up for himself, and the way BJ did him, she knew for sure he wasn't the thug he portrayed to be.

Sitting on her bed, Liyah was distraught about the pregnancy. She needed her man back and she was plotting hard to get him. She had to get rid of Mo because she was just a distraction but her biggest problem was now *Camery.* It was something about the way BJ looked at her when he spoke. Liyah saw the chemistry between them and knew in a matter of time, she may be replaced. For the last few weeks, Papi had been spending time with Camery. Liyah wasn't a fool. She searched every social site in hopes to find Camery but always came up empty. What she did find was a receipt from a credit card purchase in BJ's car. She began to google the name on the receipt and after an hour, she had found Camery's address and even her next of kin's residence. Liyah didnt know what she was gonna do with the information but for now she would hold onto it.

Liyah began looking through her dresser for a pair of warm pajamas and a pair of socks. It began to storm outside and she was freezing cold. She hated the weather in Miami because it would be burning up hot and the next day it could possibly rain. She went into the restroom and stepped into the warm steaming shower. Thoughts of her grandfather crossed her mind. She knew he was probably rolling over in his grave right now.

Her dreams of going to college were now ruined, however, she didn't need to go regardless. Everything she needed, she had. She had enough money to last a lifetime so what was really the point? She thought long and hard on opening up a business. She wasn't sure what she wanted to open but she needed something that would rack up lots of dough. She thought about a salon, but everyone had one. She thought of a boutique and again everyone owned one also. *A male exotic club,* She thought. There were plenty of women strip clubs in the city, but no entertainment for women. She made a mental not to talk to Cash because she had been in the game of strippclubs for years.

"Sup Stink?" Papi asked walking into the restroom as if everything was peachy. Liyah didn't bother to respond. She began to lather her towel and soap her body. He stood by the sink and watched her with lust. Despite the bullshit BJ put her through, he was still very much attracted to her.

He began peeling out of his clothes then hopped into the shower. Liyah pretended to be unmoved by his presence, but her heart was pounding rapidly. Everytime Papi was near her, her heart fluttered. His touch, his scent, even his aggressiveness drove her crazy.

Liyah continued to scrub her body and didn't bother to utter one word to him. He stood behind her trying to find the right things to say. He knew Liyah wasn't feeling him right now so he was gonna try everything to get in her good graces.

"I love you Liy Liy."

"Sure you do BJ."

"I do man. Don't do that."

"Do what? You talking a good one, but your actions show differently."

"I'm ready to start over."

"Sure you are."

"Stop doing that. I'm serious."

"So what you're gonna do about yo little bitch you been spending time with?"

"Who Camery?"

"Nigga you know exactly who."

"She ain't nobody ma. Im through with Mo so its just us now." he said and rubbed his hands down her back. He began kissing her neck as the water cascade down his backside. He knew what he was doing, because he knew Liyah's body couldn't resist him. *He think he so slick.* She thought. He wasn't off the hook with this Camery girl, but right now, she needed his loving so her body became submissive to his touch.

The next night...

Liyah slid into her black tights, a black t-shirt and a black hooded sweatshirt. She laced her black Jordans up and grabbed the glock that Cash had given her. *I ain't no killa but don't push me* were Liyah's thoughts as she made her way out of her bedroom. After the intense sex she had with BJ last night, she was determined to get her baby back. She had come up with a plan to get rid of both, Monique and Camery, she just prayed her plan would go smoothly. In the process she asked god to forgive her for what she was about to do, as she used her hand to crucify herself.

With everything she was dealing with, she was tired of crying so her pain only turned her into a savage. It was like, she had come out of her shell and was now on a rise of destruction. A part of her didn't want to let Cash down, but she knew Cash would understand. Speaking of Cash, she was sitting at the table fumbling through some paperwork as Liyah came into view.

When Liyah made it by the table, she tried to quickly walk past. For a brief moment, her and Cash locked eyes and it was as if Cash could read her. With out any words, Liyah headed out the home and made her way to the car.

Nearly an hour later, she pulled up to the yellow home and she was happy it was only one level. She got out of her car and crept around back quickly. Peeking through each window, she finally found what she was looking for. She could see the flickering of a television through the open window but there was a screen attached.

After removing the screen, Liyah quickly hopped through and sat in the chair like a deranged woman. Moments later, her victim had entered the room but she still hadn't noticed the woman sitting in her bedroom. Liyah's blood began to boil because Camery was wearing a red lingerie two piece, which told Liyah she was expecting company. Knowing that more than likely it was Papi, Aaliyah became Infuriated.

Finally looking over, Camery's first reaction was dive towards her bed to grab her desert eagle, but she wasn't quick enough.

"Not so fast bitch." Liyah spat knowing what she was reaching for. During Liyah's google search, it stated Camery was a Veteran in the US Military so Liyah made sure to move with caution.

Pop!

Liyah sent a shot into her back but Camery was still trying to reach her gun.

Pop! Pop! Pop!

Three more shots followed, and this time, she fell down to the bed slowly. Liyah walked over to Camery's body and flipped her over. She was bleeding from her mouth, so her cries were distinct. The frown on her face told Liyah that she was suffering, and that's exactly what Liyah wanted.

Pop! Liyah sent the last and final bullet to Camery's head killing her instantly. She then walked over to the window, and used her gun to break it. She wanted the murder to look like a break in, something she had seen in the movies. She made her way through the small home, then used her shirt to twist the knob. She walked out the home as if nothing ever happened.

Once Liyah was inside her car, she blew a sigh of relief. *This shit was easier than I thought.* She laughed out then started her engine. As she drove away from the scene, again she crucified herself then blew a kiss into the air. Right now she hadn't asked God to forgive her, because she would save that for after her next mission.

Chapter 40

Papi

Papi sat inside of his car for nearly thirty minutes. Over and over he dialed Camery's number but he got no answer. Thinking she may have been sleeping, he chose to give her a moment to finally respond. Her car was in the same spot as yesterday, which told him she hadn't left her home. A part of him wanted to knock but he wasn't the type to pop up on no woman. True she knew he was coming, but since she wasn't answering, he didn't want to seem thirsty.

Pulling out his phone he dialed her number, and again he got no answer. A part of him wanted to leave, but he didn't feel like the hour drive home. He was tired from trapping and like always, he had felt lazy.

Camery: *a ma ah nigga just sitting out here. Im'a leave if yo ass don't answer soon.*

After waiting another fifteen minutes, he still hadn't got a reply. *Fuck it, she got a nigga in there I'mma just whip out my strap and make em leave.* Were his thoughts as he exit the car. Walking up to the front door, Papi knocked like the police. After his third time knocking, he tried the knob and to his surprise it turned. A lirey feeling came over him, so he pulled his strap from his waistband and used his foot to kick open the wooden door. The house wasn't too big, but it was a nice size to be a two bedroom. Sticking his head in each door, there was no signs of her. Finally getting to the last door, which was Camery's room, he opened the door and nearly fainted. The sight before him was gruesome. Camery was sprawled out on her bed, still in the lingerie he had asked her to wear. Blood seeped from her mouth and head, and her bed was covered in blood which told him she was hit more than once. *Damn Cam.* He thought with a lone tear sliding down his face. His heart hurt for Camery because she was cool people. She was really sweet and he enjoyed every moment spent with her. *Damn who did this to you ma?* He asked himself shaking his head. *The video surveillance.* He quickly jumped to his feet remembering Camery had a camera facing the front door step. Often he would ask her, why she had it, and she would always reply, *military state of mind.*

Walking into the second bedroom, he knew it was where Camery kept her surveillance screen. He looked around the room, and he couldn't believe his eyes. There was over fifty guns, all sizes. There were a few military photos on the wall of her in her uniform and he studied them closely. He then zoomed into a picture of Camery at the white house. It was a picture of her standing next to the former president *Obama*. Papi shook his head melancholy.

He kissed the pictured than proceeded to his initial reason for coming into the room.

Papi walked over to the screen. The time displayed 12:40 am. He rewinded the tape and watched it closely. He quickly stopped the tape, then rewinded it slowly to pinpoint the part of a figure he had seen. The screen displayed the incident happened around at 12:18am. "Shit!" He banged his hands on the desk, because he was only 22 mins to late.

Pressing play, he watched as the figure used one hand to pull his sleeve over his other hand. He then used his shirt underneath his hoodie to twist the knob. Once the killer was out the house, he made the mistake of turning around to close the door behind him. Papi paused the tape then zoomed in. The killer wore all black, and the hoodie didn't do any justice. "Stinka?" he asked unsurely, but sure. He knew Liyah from anywhere and this was indeed her. He quickly ejected the tape and stuffed it into his back pocket. He used his jacket to wipe down the screen and anything else he might have touched. He quickly left the home and hopped on the freeway in deep thought. He couldn't believe Liyah would do such a thing. She wasnt no killer, shit she was barely street. But these days, he couldn't underestimate a woman scorned.

After driving around for a few hours, Papi finally headed home. After what he witnessed tonight, he was still dazed. A dead body wasn't shit to him, however, it was who the body belonged to that traumatized him. He couldn't believe Camery was now dead. Thoughts of her pretty face flashed across his mind. Her smile was bright and her bubbly personality filled his thoughts. The part that tripped him out most, was Liyah. She had turned her into a straight killer and a part of him knew what she was capable of now.

Pulling up to his home, Papi sighed and killed his engine. After a few moments of being dazed, he hopped out and made his way inside. It was now almost four in the morning so the entire house was pitch black. He headed upstairs to his room, but he stopped when he made it by Liyah's door. He pushed it open and she was sleeping as if nothing had ever happened. He walked closer to her bed and with one look at her, it pained him. She had tear stains on her cheeks that were now dried up. Her hair was untamed and she was now wearing one of Papi's white tees. He removed his shoes, followed by his clothing then climbed in the bed next to her. She began to stir in her sleep as he wrapped his arm around her. Before he closed his eyes, he leaned up and kissed her head then laid down to finally go to sleep.

When Papi opened his eyes the bright sun beamed through the window. The white sheer curtain blew slightly from the breeze. His sleep had clouded his mind so he began to wonder, was it all a dream? Liyah was now laying face to face with him.

Her eyes were wide open and she wore a somber look. Papi nor Liyah spoke one word as they stared into each other's eyes. Papi's eyes displayed a sad boy that had been disobedient. Not only was he caught up about Camery being dead, he was hurt beyond measure knowing he had pushed Liyah to that point. Many of times he had told Liyah if she stepped out, that he would body the nigga she chose, and now the tables have turned.

Papi pulled Liyah on top of him and instantly his dick grew in his briefs. He roughly kissed her as he lifted her shirt over her head. She was so turned on at the moment, everything from last night had left her mind. Her only focus right now was the love making her and Papi were about to indulge in. Looking into his eyes, it was something about the way he looked at her that made her feel *he knew*. Sliding out of his draws, he continued to kiss Liyah passionately. Though they had sex many of times, something about today felt different. The way he handled her body was like he missed her in a sense. Sliding into her wet opening, Papi noticed a difference in her love box. It was warm and tight and he was already precumming prematurely. He gripped her thighs and he guided her up and down. The feeling was so good he bit his bottom lip continuously.

"You love me don't you?" Papi asked knowing the answer. Liyah shook her head yes but that wasn't good enough.

"Tell me you love me Liyah."

"I love you Papi." she moaned out while rotating her hips. She threw her head back and closed her eyes, taking in the moment. Papi watched her in lust; she was too damn sexy. Being inside of Liyah was like entering heaven's gates. She was his angel and he danced with her on the clouds. In his entire life he had never felt a feeling so good and right now he knew he couldn't lose this feeling.

Looking deeply into her eyes, it finally registered that Liyah was the one to complete him. Getting caught up in the hype of the streets is the reason behind Liyah's demise. He regretted ever hurting her, and from this day forward he was gonna put that smile on her face he loved so much.

Chapter 41

The Beauty

"Pushhhh!" the doctor stood over Cash coaching her to push. She was in so much pain, that she cried with every push. She looked over at Braxton with a distressed look and he too looked worried.

"Come on Beautiful, I need one good push." Braxton told her.

"It hurts." she whimpered.

"I know baby but she's stuck. If you don't push, your gonna cut her circulation." Braxton assured her. The thought of something happening to her child, pained her so she began to push.

"On the count of three I need one big push." the doctor told her.

"1, 2, 3..." Braxton counted off with the doctor.

"Arrrrr!" Cash pushed as hard as she could. Her vigina felt like it had split into two.

"We got her head!" the doctor yelled over to the nurse.

"Ms. Lopez I need a nice small push and I'm gonna pull her out."

"Okay." Cash cried.

"Ahhhh!" she pushed with every piece of strength she had left.

Just as the doctor promised, he pulled the baby out, then quickly began to suction her mouth.

"Its a girl!" the doctor smiled. "Here dad you you wanna cut the cord for me?"

Braxton walked over and began clipping the umbilical cord. Thinking he would hurt her, he was a bit nervous. He looked over at Cash and she was still trying to catch her breath. Once he was done, the doctor took the baby to a nurse and began cleaning her off.

The sound of her baby crying, made Cash cry along with her. She watched as the nurse roughly cleaned her off. Once she was done, she handed the naked baby girl to Cash, placing her on her chest. The feeling of her baby girl laying on her, made her cry more.

Cash watched in awe as her heart beat soothed her precious baby. She began to rub her hands through her hair and Braxton stood on the side a proud father.

"She's beautiful." Braxton smiled widely. She had a hair full of hair, and the prettiest big eyes ever. Looking at her baby's fingertips, told Cash that she would have a nice almond complexion. When Cash noticed the deep dimple, she cooed.

"Hold her." Cash told a nervous Braxton. This was his first child, so he was a bit shaken. Though he was a doctor, the feeling was slightly different. His babygirl was a precious jewel.

"Thank you Cash." Braxton looked over to Cash. This was the happiest day of his life. For so

many years, Braxton was in love with Cash, even before he had rescued her. Until this day, deep down inside, he knew she didn't love him as much as he loved her, but he was happy she bared his child.

Braxton knew Cash loved and missed Brooklyn, and many nights it pained him. Now him and Cash had created something that would bond them forever, however he prayed this would make her fall in love.

Three Years later….

"Mommy! daddy won't give me juice." Skylar ran over to her mother.

"You have to eat first baby."

"I no eat. Its nasty." skylar complained about the broccoli Cash had pilled on her plate.

"Its good for you baby."

"No, I don't eat." Skylar folded her arms stubbornly.

"Okay well here." Cash passed her the cup of juice. Skylar was Cash's weakness, and the three year old child took advantage of it.

"That's why she's spoiled now. You can't give her anything she wants. Braxton said snatching the juice from Skylar. Skylar began to cry which pissed Cash off.

"Let's go to your room baby. Lets leave daddy because he mean." Cash pouted along with Skylar

to win her over. Braxton shook his head as the two got up from the dinner table. They headed down the hall into Skylar's room and Cash began to pull out her clothes to prepare her for her bath.

"Budder." Skylar pointed to the picture of BJ that was on her dresser.

"Yes brother baby." Cash smiled sadly.

Often Cash thought about BJ and it pained her each time. BJ was her world and until this day, she would cry. Just looking at his picture, her eyes began to weld up with tears. She missed her son dearly which was the reason she didn't mind having another child.

"No twry mommy. Otay, no twry." Skylar grabbed Cash's face as if she was the mother. Cash couldn't help but laugh, because her baby girl was to much at such a young age. It was crazy because she was a split image of BJ and even had his personality.

"Okay baby. Mommy no cry." Cash smiled at Skylar then swooped her up from the bed. She kissed her a million times, then gently hugged her.

"I love you Skylar." Cash whispered into her baby's ear.

Chapter 42

Cash Lopez

The CookOut…

Cash moved around the kitchen preparing the last of the deviled eggs. She had prepared one hundred eggs in total, along with potato salad, beans and mac and cheese. Kellz was on the grills, because he swore he was the *grill master*. She couldn't wait to taste these immaculate ribs he boasted about. They had bought, 10 slabs of ribs, 20 pounds of crab, 50 lobster tails and too much chicken to count. All though they weren't expecting to many guest, Cash loved seafood so she would be eating on it for the next few days.

Walking outside, Cash noticed that Breelah and Que had just arrived. It was something about Que that Cash couldn't quite put her finger on, but she would always let it slide. For some reason, he was mighty distant, but she took it as, him trying to repair the relationship with Bree. Que knew about Cash and Kellz, and Cash was surprised he wasn't bugging out. She figured he wasn't in love with her anymore, which was good because that boy used to go crazy.

"Sup ma?" Que walked over and kissed Cash on the cheek.

"Hey Que." Cash smiled.

"Papi what's up?" Que spoke to BJ as he emerged from the house.

"Sup." was all Papi said and Cash noticed the tension. Que brushed it off then headed over to holla at Kellz.

Aaliyah came out of the house, and Cash couldn't help but laugh at the oversized t-shirt she was wearing on top of her bikini. She shook her head knowing that she still hadn't told Papi she was pregnant. Liyah kissed Papi on the cheek and went over to talk to Breelah. *Well at least they happy.* Cash thought smiling at her children. She was happy Liyah and Papi had finally figured out that their love was destined to be. Liyah didn't bother to speak to Kamela, but at least she wasn't tripping out.

"How you doing Ms. Cash." Cali walked over and hugged Cash.

"Boy what I tell you about calling me that." Cash smirked.

"My Bad, but shit, its just respect." he smiled.

"Ohhh yeah I'm bout to fuck about nine of these up right now." Cali rubbed his hands together referring to the deviled eggs. Cash laughed and handed him the tray.

"Take them to the table when you done boy."

"Ugh this bitch." Cash heard a voice and turned around. Venicia stood there mugging Kamela who was by the pool.

"Hey pregnant little girl." Cash smiled and rubbed her stomach.

"I'm sorry Mama Cash but you know I can't stand that hoe."

"I know honey just be on your best behavior."

"I will." Venicia kissed Cash on the cheek and walked over to Aaliyah. Cash sat back and watched the girls and she knew by their looks, they were gossiping. She couldn't help but laugh, because they were another *her and Nina*. Cash and Nina talked about everything, they were always loyal to each other and even though Nina was gone, they would always remain best friends.

Cash walked over to BJ because she could tell something was up with him. She knew her son all too well and he had something heavy on his mind.

"So what's on your mind son? And don't lie because its written all over your face."

"Its a lot ma." BJ sighed. "For starters, its this nigga." he looked over at Que. "I don't know but its something about him that rubs me wrong. You know lately I ain't been wanting to cop from Gustavo, so I been copping from him. He be acting weird and the questions he be asking me be off the wall."

"Im sure its nothing BJ. but I'll tell you, keep yo eyes open." Cash bit her bottom lip looking over at Que. she too been having that weird feeling and now she was relieved to know she wasn't the only one.

"Then there's your daughter. Her ass wild." Papi shook his head. "Her ass killed Camery ma." BJ looked at his mother for her facial expression. Cash held her mouth wide open in shock.

"I knew she was up to something the other night because her ass had on all black. I thought she was going to flatten your tires or something. Wow, I would have never thought." Cash was still astonished by the information. "Love will make you do some crazy things BJ. and you gotta remember, no matter how much Liyah seems or acts innocent, her ass was breeded by wolves. She was cut from the same type of cloth as you."

"I see now." BJ continuously shook his head.

"You ever kill someone over pops?" he asked Cash anticipating her answer.

"I didn't have too. Yo daddy killed the bitch for me."

"Huh?" BJ asked confused.

"Your brother Braylen's mother had come into my life and tried to ruin it. She showed up at the first wedding right before it got shot up. She was shot in the process. Come to find out she was pregnant with Bray. its like after that the bitch wouldn't let up. Your dad saw that he was about to lose his family, so he dead the bitch before I could."

"Damn thats some savage ass shit." BJ looked off into the air.

"She should have killed Monique instead." Cash laughed causing BJ to laugh with her. She couldn't stand Monique so she wished it had been her instead of Camery.

"Nah she know Mo aint shit. I think Camery was a threat to her."

"Well I'm glad you came to your senses because you only got one shot at a real bitch in your life. All these other hoes gonna love you for either two things. Your street status or your dick. Remember that." Cash told him truthfully. Papi nodded his head and he couldn't front, everything his mother said sounded about right.

"Yeahhhh, Macita taste a piece of this rib." Kellz boasted walking over to Cash. He shoved a piece into her mouth and waited for her reaction.

"Ohh this is good." Cash savored the taste then playfully licked the sauce from his fingers.

"Yeah okay I got something you could suck on."

"Man y'all gay." Papi shot and walked off. Cash and Kellz laughed at his remark.

"Told you yo nigga could cook."

"Thats what I'm talking bout, my baby sexy and could cook, I just might marry you."

"Yeah right." Kellz laughed. Deep down inside he wished the statement was true but he wasn't gonna push it.

Cash wrapped her arms around his waist and inhaled the scent of his cologne. She slowly guided him over to the pool as she continued to kiss him. Before he knew it, she pushed him in. She was laughing hysterically but before she knew it, she too was being shoved in. She went to the bottom and quickly came back up. She wiped the water from her face and looked to see who had pushed her in. Papi stood there with a grin plastered on his face as everyone laughed.

"Awe you a trader BJ!" Cash shouted but laughing.

BJ did a cannonball into the water and Cash tackled him. As her and BJ wrestled, Kellz crept up then lifted her into the air and dunked her. They all began wrestling as everyone looked on laughing. Liyah wanted so bad to help Cash but she was too scared because of her tummy. Breelah then dived in to help her and they all began to play fight. They were having the time of their life; Until….

Chapter 43

Still at the Cookout

"Cash." a voice called out to Cash as she wrestled with Kellz. She looked over and froze.

"Mommyyy!" another voice that was all too familiar called out knocking her from her daze.

Mommy? Papi thought puzzled.

Still shocked, Cash walked over to the stairs and climbed out of the pool. Looking at Braxton, he wore a look she couldn't read. Skylar ran over and hugged her leg tightly.

"Hey baby." Cash picked her up and hugged her tightly.

"Where you been? I missed you." a six year old Skylar asked.

"Mommy been busy baby. I'm glad to see you." Cash smiled as she pinched her cheek.

"Well it sure doesn't look like it, being that its been months and you haven't come home."

"Don't you dare Braxton. You know I love my daughter." Cash spat.

If it was one thing Braxton knew, and that was, Cash loved Skylar dearly. The statement came from anger because she hadn't been back home.

Papi walked over to where Cash and Skylar stood. Everyone was taken aback by what had just transpired.

"BJ this is your sister Skylar." Cash told BJ as he approached them. Papi didn't bother to say a word, because he too was astounded.

"BJ? My brother name is BJ." Skylar said confused.

"This is your brother Sky."

"My brother die mommy."

"He's not dead anymore baby." Cash assured her.

"You want some cookies Skylar?" Breelah walked over and took Sky from Cash's arms. She knew things could get heated and she didn't want Skylar in the midst of everything. Breelah walked into the house followed by Aaliyah.

"What's going on bae?" Kellz asked making matters worse.

"Bae?" Braxton asked confused. Kellz looked from Braxton to Cash then back to Braxton.

"Who are you?" Kellz asked looking over at Braxton.

"Im her fiance. You know, the one she's been living with nearly twenty years." Braxton rubbed it in his face.

"Well I'm the nigga she's with now." Kellz stood his ground.

Cash looked on at the two and she was shocked. She knew Braxton wasn't street, but he surprised her because he wouldn't back down.

"Man this shit crazy." Papi stormed into the house.

"BJ!" Cash called out but he didnt bother to turn around.

"So is this what you've been doing while you had me and *our* child a million fucking miles away?"

"Braxton its not what you…."

"Fuck you mean its not what he thinks? Its exactly what he thinks." Kellz spat. "Yo you foul ma. You press me over my fucking wife, but you got a whole ass finance and a fucking daughter stashed away."

"Bab...Kelly." Cash quickly corrected herself. Kellz shot her an evil glare and could only shake his head.

"Man fuck you." Kellz stormed into the house.

"So you say fuck your family for some thug Cash?"

"No I didn…"

"You basically abandoned us. Were you just gonna leave us out there while you started a new life back here with your old life?"

"I wasn't gonna leave my baby!" Cash yelled now annoyed.

"So I guess its fuck me huh?" Braxton's voice softened. He knew deep inside Cash wasn't in love with him. He knew the types of guys she liked but he thought after their child things would have changed.

"Look Braxton, I appreciate everything you've done for me. I love you and I love my daughter….

"But?" Braxton interrupted knowing there was a *but.*

"But, I can't go back to Cuba. my son is alive and he needs me too. I knew Skylar was okay with you but BJ, BJ had no one. Please try to understand."

"Oh I understand. You don't want me and my corny ass." Braxton looked as if he wanted to cry, but Cash didnt say a word. Braxton saw the pain in her eyes, but was it for him or simply because she had been caught? He shook his head.

"I'll be at my hotel in case you come to your senses. I'm only in town for a couple days so get your mind right Cash." Braxton began to walk away. Before he was out of arm's reach he turned around. "Oh and I'm taking my daughter back home. And she's coming, with or without you so you better enjoy her while she's here." Braxton walked out the yard not looking back.

When Cash walked into the house, Papi was sitting on the island and Skylar sat on the side of him. She was asking him so many questions, that BJ was stumbling over his words. Cash smiled at the two, as she made her way towards them.

"I'm sorry BJ." she spoke sincerely.

"We'll holla later ma. Right now you need to go holla at Kellz because I think that nigga bout to slit his wrist." BJ forced a laugh. He was upset with Cash but she had already been through enough. He wasnt gonna badger her until he heard her side of the story.

Cash walked into her room, as Kellz was fumbling through his belongings. He hadn't officially moved in, so it was easy for him to pack up. She took a seat on the bed, lost for words. As she watched him, she saw the pain in his eyes. She felt foolish, embarrassed and most of all ashamed. There was a million things running through her mind, she didn't know where to began.

"I apologize for not telling you." she spoke pensively. He didn't say one word as he continued to pack.

"Just like you always say, I'm where I wanna be Kelly." she bit her lip nervously.

"So when the fuck was you gonna tell me this shit?!" he spat angrily.

"Soon. I mean I had to tell you because eventually I would have had to bring my daughter to meet her brother. I just couldn't figure out how I was gonna get away from *him*."

"Its just crazy because you tripped out on me about my wife. You sat here and made a nigga chose, when yo ass couldn't even call me babe in front of the nigga."

"It wasn't like that. I just have to explain myself to him and before I do, I wanted to be respectful. For all he's done for me, at least I owe him that much."

"You love that nigga?" Kellz turned to look her in the eyes. He learned if there was one way to read Cash, it was always through her eyes.

"I didn't love him purposely. I grew to love him because I felt I owed it to him. Cash said now taking a seat. "When the ship blew up, he was the one that saved me. He kidnapped me from the hospital because Mario was after me. He took me and hid me out in Cuba. For the first year, I gave him a hard time because I missed my family. I couldn't eat, I couldn't sleep, hell, I cried everyday. I still cry to this day. Finally after about a year and a half, I finally slept with him. I only did it because I wanted to imagine it was Brooklyn. I needed to feel his touch." Cash began to cry but she continued. "When the realization finally kicked in that everyone was gone, I was weak and vulnerable. He had done so much for me. If it wasnt for him, I probably wouldn't be here." She studied Kellz facial expression. "After thirteen years of being with him, I got pregnant with Sky. Now I'm not gonna say I don't love Sky, but I felt I needed her to fill the void from losing BJ." tears were now pouring down her face. "All though I had Braxton, I needed someone to call my own. I had no one." she dropped her head into her hands as the tears dripped onto the carpet like a leaking faucet. Kellz heart went out to her. He knew the hard exterior Cash but over the course of time he was seeing that Cash was a woman inside. She was sensitive which fooled the hell out of him because with Nino she was a straight gangsta. Kellz understood that because everything she been through could have been the reason for her tears and for her pain but he wanted her, scratch that, he needed her to forget about the past and enjoy life. Life had basically been stripped from her but her being reincarnated was a lesson for her to *live.*

"I don't want to put the pressure on you because I know you've been through a lot. I just hate you didn't tell me ma." Kellz took a seat next to her. Cash a nigga here for you. Please don't hide or lie about shit to me. Nothing gonna ever make me hate you or judge you because most things you've done weren't intentional, and, you have a great heart. This ain't no kitty love Macita. We grown as fuck. He stood to his feet in hopes she understood every word.

"Well I guess we even." Cash stood up and matched his posture.

"So what you gonna do ma?"

"I wanna be with you, I told you that. I love you and what we share is beyond real. All though this wasn't supposed to happen, it happened and there's nothing we could do about it. My son accepts it and that's all that matters." Cash cried freely. She loved Kellz and she wanted him to understand that every word she spoke was sincere. Right now it felt as if she was dying inside, because it pained her to imagine life with out him. She had already lost the love of her life, she couldn't lose him too. Kellz was in fact, the knight and shining armor she always envisioned. He rescued her from the traumatized woman she had become. She felt safe and secure with him to the point she barely carried her gun. After so many years, he brought happiness to her. She now had her son, her daughter and all she needed to complete her was Kelly Camren.

Chapter 44

Kellz

Watching Cash cry broke Kellz down to pieces. He listened to her story and he couldn't help but feel bad for her. As bad as he wanted to be mad, he couldn't. It was the same situation as his, but much worse. He couldn't imagine having to go live with a complete stranger because *he thought* his entire family was dead. He placed himself in Cash shoes, and no lie, they didn't fit. He really couldn't imagine what she was going through but he would for sure help her overcome it.

"So what that nigga gonna do Macita?"

"Right now I don't know. He threatened to take my daughter and go back to Cuba. I can't let that happen." again she looked worried.

"Man he ain't taking her. If you want me to bag the nigga, just say it." Kellz spoke referring to killing Braxton. For a moment Cash considered, but she had too good of a heart. No matter what she did, and had done in her life, it was always strictly business. She was a kind and genuine person at heart so killing Braxton was far from her mind.

"We'll worry about that later. Right now we need to get downstairs. Skylar prolly talking poor BJ's ears off." they both chuckled. Cash and Kellz both sighed silently, because they both now felt a bit of relief.

When the two made it downstairs, everyone appeared to be gone except, Breelah and Que. Papi was still seated with Sky and Liyah sat across from them. Kellz walked over to the bar and through back two shots as Cash interrupted a babbling Skylar.

"Mommy, my brother is the coolest." Sky beamed. Cash couldn't help but laugh, because she was wearing Papi's chain.

"I love aunty Breeya too. Oh and Stinka." she looked over at Liyah. Everyone burst out laughing.

"What about me Sky?" Que asked feeling left out.

"You too. wus yo name again?" she put her finger on her forehead as if she was thinking.

"Uncle Que."

"Oh yeah Que." she giggled "Que is cute." she smiled.

"Girl what you know about somebody being cute?" BJ asked laughing

"I always hear mommy call daddy cute. Huh mommy?" Skylar giggled. "Stinka cute too." she looked over at Liyah. Everyone burst out laughing. Skylar was too much and she got it honest.

"Thank you Skylar." Liyah blushed.

"You welcome."

"Mommy, BJ not dead so where my abuelita? She not dead too?" her smart ass asked. Everyone was silent at the question, and chose to let Cash answer.

"Honey your abuelita not here. Are you hungry?" Cash quickly changed the subject.

"Yes starving." Sky rubbed her belly. Cash couldn't help but admire her, she had so much personality.

Kellz sat back and watched Skylar. He wanted so bad to introduce himself but he didn't want to rush things. Skylar was a real life doll. Her big pretty eyes, reminded him of Cash and her little sassy attitude topped it off. Her long curly hair fell down her shoulders and she was to die for, along with her dimple.

"What's your name?" Sky hopped off the couch and headed to Kellz.

"I'm Kellz lil mama."

"Are you my uncle or my brudda?"

"Ha ha yeah I'm your uncle." Kellz chuckled.

"Well hello uncle Kell." she beamed. She then walked out the house in search of Cash so she could get her plate.

"Man that girl gonna be a hand full." Papi laughed.

Kellz watched her closely as she headed out the door. He began to wonder what would life be like if he and Cash bared a child. He knew she probably wouldn't want anymore, but shiddd, Kellz was determined to put a baby in her. Having Sky around, made Kellz feel even better. Now that she was here, Cash had no reason to leave. Kellz was gonna do everything in his power to help Cash with her family, and he promised himself to never let her down.

Monique

Monique was in her shop, trying her best to concentrate on her client. Every since the day she left Papi, he hadn't called nor returned her calls. She knew Cash played a big part in it, and that shit had pissed her off. She was still shocked Cash was alive, and a part of her wished she was still dead.

"Mo the police are out front in riot gear!" Arcelie ran over nervously.

"What they want?" Mo stopped attending to her client and began to panic. All though she hadn't done anything wrong, she was still nervous. *Maybe its Papi they looking for,* she thought walking over to the picture window. Before she could get a good view, the door came crashing in and about fifty officers swarmed the salon.

One office ran over to Mo, and quickly apprehended her. He then nodded to the other officers, as if he had his man. Monique stood puzzled but she remained calm.

"May I ask what is this about?" she asked the officer that led her out the door.

"I'm going to need you to stand out here for me. A sargent will be over to talk to you." he spoke calmly then headed back into the salon. Another officer had approached them and asked the officer standing next to Mo, "have you searched her car?"

"Berkleys doing it now." the officer assured his partner.

Moments later, a few officers walked over holding a gun inside of a plastic bag. Mo was stunned because her gun was in the shop and it was licensed to her.

"Monique Moore, you're under arrest for the murder of Camery Jones. You have the right to remain silent…"

"What the fuck you mean murder, I haven't murdered anyone!" Mo cried out. The officers walked her over to a car and shoved her in. they continued to destroy her shop as she sat in the back of the car pitiful. She looked out the window, with tears falling from her eyes. Then it hit her, Camery was the same chick that Papi had started sleeping with. She remembered the name from the day at the restaurant. The more she thought, the more she cried. She loved Papi yes, but killing for a nigga wasn't in her character.

"You have a collect call from, its me Mela." she heard her mother's voice through the phone. Kamela quickly dialed 5 to accept.

"What you dun got yourself into now?" Kamela asked annoyed.

"I haven't did anything. Please, I need your help."

"Oh now you need me?"

"Kamela please. I need you to bail me out. My bail is a million but they only want ten percent. I have seventy thousand in my safe, and if you could, ask Papi for the rest please."

"Yeah aight." Kamela said and headed into Moniques bedroom. "What's the combination?"

"Its 08-10-19-81." she could hear the lock spinning.

"I'm in." Kamela spoke nonchalantly.

"Okay come down and post it please."

"Yeah aight. I'll be there." Kamela hung up the phone. She really didn't have much to say to Mo, and she was dumb if she thought this was gonna make her jump.

Kamela began to count out the seventy thousand, and what tripped her out, was, there was five times the amount. *This bitch got all this money but she wants Papi to help out. I guess she wanna feel important.* Kamela thought as she counted through the rest of the money. By the time she was done, she had counted well over four hundred thousand. Shaking her head, Kamela rushed to her room and grabbed a duffle bag. She ran back into the room and tossed every last dollar into the bag. She quickly headed out the house, ignoring the initial reason she had come.

She was actually here to get her clothes so she could take them to her dad's home. Since she had been there, Que pretty much purchased her a new wardrobe. All though she had new clothing, there were still some important things she wanted from home.

Kamela hopped on the freeway, and drove out two hours away. She dumped Que's Benz on the side of the road and caught a cab the rest of the way.

By the time she made it to her destination, she was happy to be out of dodge. She walked into the facility, straight to the counter.

"Yes may I help you?"

"Yes I wanna purchase a one way ticket to California."

"I could help you with that. Do you have your ID?"

"Yes." Kamela pulled out her ID and handed it to the attendant.

After purchasing her ticket, she took a seat and waited for her bus. *Dumb bitch.* She thought of Monique, because she had just robbed her blind. Kamela was going to California to start another life, and she was four hundred thousand dollars richer.

"You have a collect call from *Monique*." the caller spoke. Papi pulled the phone away from his ear shocked. He pressed five and patiently waited for Mo to speak.

"Papi."

"Yeah."

"I need your help. I'm in jail and I need to be bailed out. Kamela was suppose to be here hours ago but she hasn't showed up. Please if you can come get me and I'll pay you back when I catch up with her, she has all the money."

"Why you didn't call that nigga Que. I mean ain't that the last dick you had in your mouth?"

"What are you talking about?"

"Bitch you know what I'm talking about. He sent me the video of you blowing his socks back. So call that nigga hoe and have him come get you." Papi spat.

"Nigga I'm here because of you. I know you killed Camery and framed me. Watch Ima have yo ass." Mo shouted then disconnected the line.

Monique was beyond crushed by his words but she couldn't blame him. The day Que had come over, she did in fact suck him off but she didn't think he would stoop as low as to sending the video. She now felt like shit as she cried her eyes out. She was in jail for the murder of a bitch Papi was fucking and now she had to reap the benefits of it.

She knew she couldn't tell the authorities on Papi, because she wouldn't last five minutes on the streets; he would for sure kill her. The officers had took her into interrogation three times but she chose to remain silent. Kamela hasn't showed up, and she wasn't surprised. However, she took it as she was busy and would be coming soon. She sat down on the cold steel and said a silent prayer. Tears flowed from her eyes, because just that fast, her life was caving in.

Chapter 45

Cash Lopez

Cash and Kellz laid on the sofa watching television as Kellz rubbed his hands through her hair. She felt a sense of relief that Kellz had chose to stick around and accept the skeleton that she had kept hidden. Not to mention BJ. Last night she had a talk with BJ and told him everything from the day the ship blew up, up until the day Braxton had received the call about survival. Her and BJ were in good standings and she loved how he bonded with his sister. With BJ still living and Skylar now in Miami, Cash felt complete.

"Mom help!" BJ yelled from the living room. Cash lifted from Kellz embrace and the two of them headed into the living room. When they walked in, they couldn't help but laugh because BJ was struggling with bags, as Skylar played with a Barbie.

"Oh my BJ."

"Its more." BJ said and nodded his head outside.

Cash walked to the door, and all she could do was shake her head.

"Papi!" she shouted in a unbelievable tone. Papi had rented a uhaul truck and she could only imagine what was in it.

"That's her man, she wanted everything." Papi shrugged his shoulders as Kellz laughed.

Kellz and Cash walked to the uhaul and looked inside. There were bikes, two doll houses, plenty bags from toys r us and many other bags from gucci, saks and many more stores.

"My brother bought me a lottt of stuff." Sky smiled adding emphasis.

"Ms. Lopez." John walked over just in time.

"Hey John could you get someone to help bring these things in?"

"Yes ma'am. Also the gentleman is back." he gave Cash and uneasy look.

"What gentlemen?"

"The one that showed up with the baby." John looked over to Skylar. Knowing he was talking about Braxton, Cash sighed.

"Let him in." she said and walked into the home. She knew what he was there for but over her dead body was he gonna take her child.

Kellz and Papi followed Cash into the home. Moments later, Braxton appeared with his nose turnt up. He eyed Kellz then focused his attention to Cash.

"So I'm guessing you decided to stay?" Braxton asked sounding like a complete asshole. Cash couldn't believe this side of him, because back home he was the sweetest man ever.

"Yeah she staying and Sky staying to." Kellz jumped in. He was tired of Braxton and his fake gangster attitude. He saw right through Braxton's corn ball ass, and he knew he wouldn't throw a crayon in a kindergarten riot.

"Its none of your concern. And my daughter is going home. I'll be damned if I leave her here to be raised by thugs." Braxton spat.

"I'll show you a thug." Kellz whipped out his pistol. Braxtons eyes grew wide and he was scared shitless.

"Look, before I whip my strap out on you too, I'd advise you to shake the spot. My mom's been through enough. We hadn't seen each other in twenty fucking years and not to mention this my first time meeting my little sister. Now Ima need you to hop back on the first boat to Cuba, Doogie Howser, before I send you back floating." Papi spoke calmly. All though Papi was calm, everyone standing in his presence knew he wasn't playing. He looked from Papi to Cash, then looked at his daughter who was busy playing with her new toys.

"Skylar." Braxton called out to her.

"Yes daddy?"

"Daddy is going back home doll."

"Okay daddy. I wanna stay with mommy. You promise you gonna come back right?" she asked with her hands on her hips.

"Yes I promise." Braxton replied as he nodded his head. He looked as if he wanted to break down and cry and no lie it was a sad moment. He headed towards the door, then turned back around. He took one last look at Cash, and quickly dropped his head.

The sound of Cash's phone ringing from the den made her look off. She went to get it, in hopes it was Breelah. Tonight her and Bree were going out to eat and she had been waiting for her call for hours. Lately Bree had been under Que so Cash hadn't seen much of her. She missed Bree to death but she also was enjoying her time with Kellz. After today, an outing was much needed. As bad as she wanted to feel bad for Braxton, she couldn't. Braxton knew deep down Cash was with him because of obligation, so she didn't understand why he was acting in such a way. She didn't ask to be there, and plenty times she told him she was leaving back to Miami.

Kellz soon walked into the den in hopes of getting back cozy with his girl. But It was something about the look she wore as she listened to the caller.

"Don't mention this to anyone, I'll be there." Cash said then disconnected the line. She took a seat on the sofa and went into a straight trance.

"Baby what's wrong now?" Kellz asked worried.

"I have to take a trip."

"A trip? When and where?"

"I'll explain it later." she lifted from the couch and headed to her room. The old Cash was back, and it was time she suit up.

---

10 hours later, Cash and Kellz had pulled up to the location. Kellz looked over at Cash and chuckled lightly to himself. She was rocking a one piece black catsuit and a pair of black thigh high boots looking sexy. What tripped him out, was, she was on a killing mission but looking sexy as hell. She joked and laughed with him all through her mind was elsewhere. The sound of Nino's voice played in Kellz head, and all he could do was laugh at the memory. *Man Cash a straight beast Kellz. We going to kill shit and Lil Mama be playing Jay Z and Beyonce and acting all regular. Shit I think I was more worried than her.* And now Kellz knew exactly what he meant.

Kellz and Cash, headed into the large home. He wondered how the hell were they gonna get inside not knowing it was all premeditated. Cash had told Kellz about the hit, but she failed to mention who had initially called her.

When they walked up to the porch, the door was already ajar. Cash walked in slowly and her caller was sitting on the couch.

"Where is she?" Cash asked quietly.

"The back, fourth door to the left."

Cash walked down the long hall, leaving Kellz behind. When she made it to the fourth door, she pulled out her gun, and slowly opened the door.

"Well hello Gabriela." Cash taunted walking into full view. Gabriela who's back was facing the door, turned around and got the shock of her life.

She knew Cash Lopez all too well, so she knew the reason for her visit wasn't a pleasant one. She also thought about the time she sent Nino the tape of Cash and Carter sharing a kiss, so she was more than sure Cash hated her guts.

"Uhh..Ca...Cash what are you doing here?" she asked shaken. Gabby, just as everyone else thought Cash was dead, so seeing her here in the flesh had her not only scared but appalled.

"You know why I'm here. I owe yo ass anyway from sending my husband that tape. But this here is much more personal bitch!" Cash lifted her firearm and walked near Gabby.

"This how this is gonna go. You're gonna drink this entire bottle." Cash said and held up a bottle with its contents. "And if you don't, Ima gonna shoot you with every bullet I have in this gun." Cash handed Gabby the bottle, and she looked petrified. When Cash saw the hesitance in her face, she raised her firearm ready to shoot. Gabby quickly drank the substance, as tears poured from her eyes. Cash looked down at her watch, then back to Gabby.

"You have about three minutes." Cash smirked.

Exactly three minutes later, Gabby dropped to her knees fighting for her life. She clutched her throat but there was nothing she could do. Just as she had killed Carter, she was gonna die.

"You live by the sword, you die by it. Tell Carter I'll see him when I get there." Cash spoke as

Gabby took her last breath. Gabby collapsed to the floor, and died instantly. Cash checked her pulse. Satisfied with the results, she walked out to talk to Keisha.

"Wrap her up." Cash tossed Kellz the plastic wrap then walked over to take a seat. She looked at Keisha and saw the fear in her eyes but she was gonna spare her. Kellz walked to the back of the house to begin the wrap.

"I'm not gonna kill you." Cash assured her. "I know we haven't seen eye to eye but I'm willing to let it go. I really appreciate you calling me." Cash spoke truthfully.

"There's more." Keisha spoke nervously. Keisha had told Cash how Que and Gabriela killed Carter. She promised Cash she had nothing to do with it and how she had overheard them talking about it.

"Que was also the reason the FEDS raided when Blaze and Tiny were killed. He had made a deal with the FEDS and got paid plenty money. I'm sorry I never told you but I was in love with him."

"So what made you tell now?"

"He brought me here thinking we were gonna be a family. He married Gabriela and basically had us both living here. I wasn't really tripping, but then he left to Miami. I saw a instagram post of Breelah and him, and that told me why he hadn't been back. I saw a pic of you and Breelah and that's how I knew you were still alive." Keisha dropped her head shamefully.

"So you guys been living in Carter's house as if it was nothing."

"Well I never knew it was Carter's house. I never even knew Gabriela was Carter's wife."

"Wife?" Cash asked appalled.

"Yes they were married." Cash couldn't believe her ears. He was married to Lydia, who was also killed along with her children on the ship. She shook her head because this was a complete shock.

"Let's roll ma." Kellz said emerging from the back. Cash nodded her head then looked back to Keisha.

"I'm gonna send someone to get her body." Cash looked at a shaken Keisha.

"Well I don't think Ima be here."

"Oh okay. So do you have somewhere else to go?"

"Well my daughter is in college. I have an apartment near her campus. When I saw Breelah was still living, I knew Que was gonna go back to her so I pretty much packed up and left. I'm done with him Cash." Keisha spoke between tears. Cash shook her head, in agreeance.

"Well that should be enough to keep you on your feet." she handed Keisha a duffle bag.

Looking into the bag, Keisha's eyes grew wide. There was all hundred dollar bills, neatly stacked.

"Thank you." she looked at Cash pleadingly. The two hugged, and Cash informed her that if she ever needed anything to reach out. Cash let the beef between them go. Que was a complete monster and

Keisha was innocent in it all. Not to mention, she loved Qui and wanted nothing but the best for them.

Cash and Kellz left the home. Now knowing that Que had bargained with the FEDS had Cash distraught. Out of all people, she couldn't believe her ears. She knew now what she had to do, and that was to send Que home to his maker. He didn't deserve to live another moment, but she would simply watch him until it was her time to strike.

Chapter 46

Breelah

"Stop Que!" Breelah laughed out as Que wrestled her down to the bed. The two had been cooped up in their home. Breelah had cooked up a hearty meal and they were now in their room, enjoying each others company. This was the first time they were alone in the home because Kamela was always around. Its been a week since Kamela been gone, which had Que slightly worried. Last he had heard, she ran off with her mother's money, and she had even changed her number. Monique had called Que asking if he could bail her out, and just as Papi, he laughed, then disconnected the call.

"Hello?" Breelah answered her ringing phone.

"Breelah, don't make things obvious, but are you with Que?"

"Yes Im home." Breelah played it off.

"I need you to make up an excuse to get away from him. Hes foul as fuck and I'll tell you about it when you get here. For the most part, he's the one who killed Carter."

"Okay I'll see you soon." Breelah tried her hardest to hold her composure. She looked at Que and nearly threw up her whole stomach. She disconnected the line with Cash, and now her whole thought process had been thrown off.

"I..I have to go." Breelah quickly lifted off the bed. Que grabbed her arm and spent her around.

"Wait. I thought we was chilling till later ma. You promised I could put a baby in you." Que laughed.

"Ummm..Umm...Cash needs me to keep Sky." she lied.

"Oh okay." Que responded unsurely. A part of him told him, Bree was lying but he let it ride.

"Aight baby, well I'll see you later. I gotta go handle some shit anyway." he kissed her on the cheek.

Breelah slid into her shoes and headed out the house. She wanted so badly to grab her belongings but she didn't want to alarm him. She hopped into her car and began crying instantly. She would have never thought in a million years her brother would have been dead, and behind the hands of Que. She thought after the first incident, that things had died down, but she thought wrong. When Carter disappeared, she expected him to be hiding out. Everyday she thought about him and prayed he'd appear, but, he never did. Her gut feeling told her, her brother was dead, but because he faked his first death, she had hope.

I sat on the ship the day of Cash's wedding praying to God Que would show up. Que and I hadn't spoke because of the beef him and my brother Bronx had. I was now pregnant, and wanted to tell Que but he never showed up. The ship had sailed off, and now I was really sad. I watched as everyone was in a good mood and celebrating. I was happy for Cash and Brooklyn, but I had so much on my mind, I couldn't keep up with the celebration.

After we left the bahama's for the ceremony, we were back on the ship for the reception. Everyone were enjoying them self and suddenly... Boom! I heard a loud bang, and instantly it knocked me into the water. I was burned down the whole side of my body, but the water quickly soothe me. I fell down to what seemed like the bottom of the ocean, and I was afraid I wouldn't be able to make it up. By the time I swim back up, I was out of breath and on the verge of passing out. I looked around the water and their were so many bodies sprawled out. The boat was now on fire, and all I could do was cry.

Breelah pulled up to Cash's house and jumped out the car hurriedly. When she walked in, she headed to find Cash. Finding her in the den, she began asking a million questions.

"So from what I know, Que and Gabriela killed Carter. Gabriela poisoned him."

"Wait Gabriela? The Brazilian chick Bronx was dating?"

"Yes. apparently she's Que's wife now."

"So my brother is dead?" Bree plopped down on the sofa. Tears poured from her eyes and her hands shook profoundly.

"And they were living in his house." Cash added.

"That muthafucka."

"And there's more." Cash looked over to make sure Bree was paying full attention.

"He made a deal with the FEDS and gave up the empire. He didn't tell on me, but he basically gave up Blaze. That's why the FEDS raided Blaze and Tiny's home.

"I can not believe him. But why Blaze?"

"I don't know. That's the part that has me confused." Cash added now joining Bree on the sofa. Breelah couldn't believe her ears. She knew it was something about him that was off. He was acting weird, and even secretive.

"So what now?"

"You already know." Cash shot Breelah a disturbed look.

"He has to die." Breelah spoke just above a whisper. Cash nodded her head yes.

Chapter 47

Papi

Papi drove out two and a half hours away from home. He was on his last brick of work and needed to re-up pronto. Finally making it to Gustavo's mansion, he was let into the gate by security, he made his way up the driveway. When he stepped out the car, he was met by four guards who escorted him into the home. Upon entering the home, the guards searched him and stripped him from the firearm he had in his waistband. Papi never understood why Gustavo did all this. It wasn't like he could kill them with one gun and make it out alive. Papi didn't sweat it though, because he understood in this game, no one could be trusted.

Papi was escorted to the back where Gustavo waited at his conference table. There were two guards inside the room, which caused Papi to shake his head. Mean mugging the guard at the door, Gustavo began to laugh. He always told Papi he had heart, which was the reason he began doing business with him. Often Gustavo asked Papi to become a part of his team, but Papi would always decline. Papi was his own man and had just as much money as Gustavo.

"Papi my boy, how's it going?"

"Sup Gustavo. You know what I'm here for so let me get my shit and roll."

"Ha ha ha, still crazy I see. You know you remind me of your mother so much."

"You know you tell me that everytime I'm here."

"So where have you been because I don't see you long time?"

"Shit I had been copping work from Que. A nigga be tired of this long ass drive. And he..

"Que as in Quintin?" Gustavo cut Papi off.

"Yeah."

"So he's back around?"

"Yeah you know he fucks with my aunt." Gustavo began shaking his head. He knew Que all too well and Que was poison. Because of the love for Ms. Lopez, Gustavo was gonna let Papi in on a few things.

"You know that Pendejo works for the FEDS?"

"Hell nah not Que." Papi jumped to Que's defense. Que was a lot of things but a snitch, he wasn't.

"Who do you think sent the policia to take down the guy and his girlfriend. You know, your mother's friends."

"Blaze and Tiny?"

"Yes. mother fucker made a deal with them. I've been looking for his ass."

"With all due respect, I can't believe that one." Papi shot. Gustavo began to laugh mochly to his guards, and that shit was pissing Papi off.

"Okay you don't believe, well believe this. That bitch was the one who blew up your mother's ship for her wedding. Did you know he worked for Mario?"

"Nah."

"Well si mijo. Why do you think Mario never kill him. Mario raised Que daughter and made him leave the country." Gustavo spoke knowingly. Right then, a man entered the room with two duffel bags, and handed them to Papi. Still not believing his ears, he stood to his feet.

"Good looking Gustavo." Papi thanked him, but not for the drugs, but the information about Que. Walking to the door, Gustavo called out to Papi.

"Bring him to me Papi and your pay will be great."

"With all do respect Gu, I gotta kill that muthafucka myself. Papi spat. Gustavo nodded his head approvingly, and with that Papi was out the door.

On his ride back home, Papi's mind was in overdrive. *I knew it!* He shouted banging his hands on the steering wheel. He knew Gustavo was indeed telling the truth because how would he know about Liyah. Nobody knew that Liyah was Mario's grandchild, until the day he showed up. Not to mention, the look Mario was giving Que, didn't sit well with Papi. it was like they had some type of connection. What really made perfectly good sense was, if Mario hated his mother and grandmother's empire so much, why didn't he kill Que out of all people. Que was a top soldier, and called lots of shots. It was no puzzle that Que played a big role in the Lopez empire, so he should have been the first nigga to go. *That bitch was the one who blew up your mother's ship for her wedding.* The thought of Gustavo's voice played in his mind. He couldn't believe Que would do such a thing to people he called family. Now knowing Que was behind the death of his love ones, all hell was about to break loose.

Pulling up to his home, Papi ran into the house to his room. He slid into some black sweats and a black hoodie. He then sat down to send a text. Aaliyah came into the room, that they now shared, but she had a puzzled look. It was something about the way Papi looked, that made her know something was wrong. Not to mention, he was dressed in all black.

"Sup Stinka?" he spoke placing his phone on the dresser. He then stood up, to grab his twin desert eagles from his closet, placing them in his holsters on each sides of his hips. Aaliyah looked on and wanted so badly to tell him not to do whatever it was he was gonna do, so she thought long and hard on what to say.

"Hey I have something to tell you." she looked at him with innocent eyes.

"Sup?" Papi took a seat on the bed and Liyah did the same.

"I don't know how you're gonna feel about this but, I'm pregnant!" she blurted out.

"Word?" Papi asked astonished. As much as he wanted to be happy, he couldn't right at this moment. He needed to handle his business then he would be sure to shower Liyah with excitement.

"So Ima be a daddy? Thats whats up." he slightly smiled. "Look ma, I got some shit I gotta take care of and I promised when I get back, its me and you." he kissed her forehead.

"But what if you don't make it back?" Liyah's eyes began to water.

"I promise Ima make it back." again he kissed her then walked towards the door. "I love you Stinka, and if I don't do nothing else, Ima make it back home to you and my seed." he spoke sincerely.

"I love you Brooklyn." tears poured from her eyes. Papi hit her with that sexy grin she loved then headed out, closing the door behind him.

Noticing Papi had left his phone, Aaliyah jumped up to grab it. She went to try and catch him, to tell him he had left it, right when a text came through from Que. Aaliyah began reading the messages.

Papi: *aye unc, meet me at the yacht. I need to show you this bullshit I just copped.*

Que: *aight nephew. I'll be there in about an hour.*

But Papi never received the text. Liyah then went to the text above and began reading.

Papi: *Nigga you not gonna believe this shit.*
Young: *what happened now?*
Papi: *make a long story short, that nigga Que the one had the ship blew up*
Young: *I knew it! I fucking knew it!*
Papi: *yeah I felt it too but check it, Imma hit you in a sec, Ima go holla at the boy.*
Young: *man just let me know where*
Papi: *one*

Tears poured down Aaliyah's face as she read the text. Father or not, it was something about Que she didn't like. What really tripped her out, was she knew he had been working for her grandpa because she had seen him a few times at their home. She didnt know he was her father but he had to know which told her he didnt give a fuck about anyone. Liyah cried harder, because the look on Papi's face told her he was on a killing spree. She prayed he would indeed make it home to her and her baby. She laid back on the bed contemplating her next move. A part of her told her to let Papi handle his business then another part told her to stand by her man side.

Chapter 48

Papi

Papi pulled up to the yacht, and dead his engine instantly. He looked around for Que's car but it was nowhere insight. He made his way onto the yacht to wait patiently. When he walked on, it was pitch black so he headed over to turn on the light.

"Got damn nigga!" Papi shouted. Que was sitting on a stool, like a straight weirdo.

"What you scared little nigga?" Que asked with a grin. It was something about the way Que spoke that made him feel uneasy.

"Nah nigga, yo ass just sitting here in the dark like a creep and shit." Papi laughed to break the ice.

"What you wanted to show me?" Que asked walking closer to Papi. Papi fondled with the bag he was carrying, as if there was some work inside.

"Let me see." Que spoke walking closer. With an eerie feeling, Que had his hand on his pistol ready to dead Papi right where he stood. Sensing something wasnt right, Papi quickly pulled out his firearm but he wasnt quick enough. Que already had his weapon out, and pointed it to Papi's head.

"What you thought you was about to do?" Que asked as they both held their guns aiming them at one another. *Tackle this nigga.* Papi thought staring into the eyes of his prey.

"Man you a straight bitch. All this time, you running around acting like you love my mom's and my family, but you snaking the whole time. I knew I should have killed yo ass the night you showed up."

"Should have followed your first mind." Que smirked ready to squeeze the trigger. Papi quickly tackled him to the ground knocking both their firearms from their hands. He punched Que in the face trying to daze him, but the jab didnt work. Que flipped Papi onto his back, however it didn't last long. The two began rolling and flipping, both trying to reach for their pistols. With much force, Papi flung Que across the room, and quickly grabbed the duffle bag. Que scrambled to his feet and pulled out his second gun. Papi who wasn't able to get his gun out in time, took off running towards the deck. He quickly ducked behind the first thing that could shield him. From where he was kneeled down, he saw Que approaching. Papi quickly pulled out his gun and fired a shot but missed. Papi then ran to the other side, firing another shot. Que ducked for cover but was grazed in the hand. Papi dove, sending two shots into Que's torso. Que fell to the ground instantly, but sent off two shots in Papi's direction but missed him. When Papi walked over to Que to finish him off, Que fired again letting off three shots and the third bullet struck Papi knocking him over the ledge. Falling into the ocean, Papi floated underneath the water. When he came back up, he noticed the blood and began to panic. Que scrambled to his feet and walked over to the ledge, in search of Papi. His eyes scanned the water but Papi was nowhere in sight. Knowing he was hit, Que figured he was probably dead, and he would leave him right where he was.

"BJ!" Que heard a voice so he quickly moved to the side and ducked. Que knew the voice all too well, and it belonged to none other than *Cash*.

Chapter 49

Que

Que was in deep thought about the episode that had just transpired. He didnt want to kill Papi, out of guilt, but like he always said, *kill or be killed.* Que was no fool, it was something about the way Papi was acting that told him not to trust the young nigga. Which was the reason he was there first and sitting in the dark. His gut feeling told him, Papi was coming to kill him so he figured if he showed up first, he'd have the upper hand.

When he called his women in Brazil and got no answer, it was the first signal. Not to mention the way Breelah had ran off and had been acting lately. She had been avoiding his calls and hadn't been home since the day Cash called her. A few times he went to Cash's house in search for her, and Liyah would lie and say she wasn't there. He knew it was a lie because just as he had on Cash's phone years ago, he had a tracker on Breelah's phone as well.

The icing on the cake was, he peeped Cash following him. At first he thought he was tripping but it was confirmed when he parked at one of his secret homes, then took an emergency exit out. He watched Cash from a distance as she watched his home eagerly. Right then he knew something was up. He figured she had found out about the ship, so it was now time to handle the whole family. He was gonna start with BJ, then Breelah was next on his list, saving Cash for last. Que was eager to kill the whole family and get the empire he had been wanting for years. Now that Mario was out of the picture, it was time he made his move anyway. He was tired of pretending as if he missed everyone and wanted to start over with Bree. Deep down, Que wanted his empire, then to go back home to his women and live happily ever after. He didn't give too fucks if Liyah decided to come, because she really didn't mean shit to him after all. When he tried to repair the lost love with Liyah, it was only so he wouldn't look like the bad guy, which was why he blamed Mario. The day Liyah chose to stay with Cash, was the day she died to him. *Fuck her too.* Were his daily thoughts and he meant it.

Que stood to the side and waited for Cash to walk into view. After a few moments, she came out onto the deck with a firearm in hand. As she searched for BJ, she never saw Que approaching.

Click!

Cash felt the cold steel pressed against her head.

"Drop the gun." Que spoke clutching his womb. Cash quickly dropped the gun and Que kicked it a few feet away.

"Walk." he told her forcing her to walk back inside the yacht. Once inside, Que patted her down, but not taking his gun off her. Finding another gun, he removed it, then placed it in his pocket. Cash eased a look at Que and noticed he was covered in blood. She began to panic, not knowing if her child was okay.

"Where's BJ?"

"Tough guy swimming with the fishes." Que spoke enraged.

"You killed my son?" Cash's blood began to boil.

"Little nigga tryin play a grown man's game and failed. You know he not as sharp as you Cash."

.

"But why Que?"

"Bitch you know why. Yo ass ain't even supposed to be alive now. I killed you hoe." Que struck Cash with the gun. Cash grabbed her head, and saw specks of blood on her hand.

"So you were responsible for the explosion?" Cash asked already knowing the answer.

"You damn right. A nigga got ten mill too."

"So it was all for the money? You went against the empire for ten million dollars?

"You know damn well I didn't need the money. It was bout my empire."

"Your empire? So you did all this to take over the empire? Why didn't you just talk to me about it? I would have just passed it on to you."

"Bitch you a fucking lie. You wasn't gonna never pass the throne. You know Ms. Lopez promised that empire to me, so Imagine my surprise when she handed it to you. All that work I did getting her locked up, and she passes the fucking empire to her precious little daughter." he spoke with vengeance.

So he was responsible for my mom getting knocked. Cash thought not believing her ears.

"So you're a snitch now?" Cash taunted him.

"You damn right I'll drop a dime on any one of you muthafuckas for the money. You know Mike bitch ass could've been eating like me but that dumb ass nigga went against me and tried to make a side deal." Que laughed. "Why you think I rescued you that day he kidnapped you? I couldn't risk that bitch ass nigga telling you I was in on it. You thought I rescued you because I loved you? Bitch you crazier than I thought." he laughed tauntingly. "Yeah a nigga was in love with you when I shot that punk ass Carter, but after that, you wasn't shit to me but pussy. You know I never had no real beef with Nino, I didn't give two fucks about you and him fucking, but I knew if he came into the picture it would be harder for me to get the empire."

"Fuck you. Nigga you loved me and you loved every piece of this pussy." Cash through in his face.

"I aint gone lie, that pussy good as fuck but I love my money more. You know I was gonna actually spare you until after the whole bullshit with Carter came out. You turned yo back on me for that nigga. Whether you fucked him or not, bitch you was supposed to roll with the empire. But nah, yo dicked whipped ass just had to turn yo back on me.

So when I blew up that ship, I didn't show no remorse for you or any muthafucka on there."

"If its money you want I'll give you fifty million and you could just go on with your life."

"Bitch you think I'm dumb. Your Cash fucking Lopez, no matter where I hide I know you'll find me."

"But what about your daughter Que? Mario's already gone, she needs me."

"Fuck her. That little bitch chose you over me. I didn't want her ass anyway. You actually did me a favor by killing that hoe Stephanie, I wish y'all would've just killed that bastard bitch too."

"You just don't give a fuck about nothing huh?"

"Nope. In this game, its killed or be killed. Remember, you taught me that ma."

"So kill me then bitch. You know I'm not scared to die."

"You ain't said nothing but a word. I'll see you in…." Before Que could finish, a single shot went off, and Cash closed her eyes, waiting for her body to fall.

Thump!

The sound of Que's body hit the ground. Cash quickly turned around and Que was laying on the floor with a bullet to the head. She looked towards the door and she couldn't believe her eyes.

"Liyah?" she asked with tears pouring down her face.

Chapter 50

Aaliyah

Liyah lifted the hoodie from off her head and looked at Cash pleadingly. The two held each other's gaze for what seemed like eternity. Cash couldn't believe her eyes. Liyah had murdered her own father for her, and that shit made Cash's heart cry out. She knew now that Liyah was destined to be in her life, and she would always love her as her own child.

Liyah also heard Que speak on Cash killing her mother, but right now that wasn't here nor there. Cash ran to Liyah and hugged her so tight, the two began crying in each other's arms.

After the intense moment, Liyah pulled back and handed Cash the gun.

"You have to finish him off mommy." Liyah told Cash looking at Que's body. Wasting no time, Cash walked over to Que's body, and sent four more bullets into his body. Two into his head, and two into his chest. Cash then turned to Liyah and the thought of BJ being dead began to take a toll on her.

"BJ's dead." Cash cried looking at Liyah.

"Nooo please don't tell me that." Liyah began to cry.

"We have to go find his body. We can't just leave him here." Cash grabbed Liyah's arm and pulled her towards the entrance.

Walking down the dock, Cash noticed a figure struggling for his life. The figure had come from out the water, and rolled over on his back. When Cash got closer to the figure, she could see his chest heaving up and down as if he was desperately trying to catch his breath.

"BJ?" she cried realizing it was her child. She kneeled down beside him and cried as hard as she could.

"Oh my god BJ!" the tears poured from her eyes.

"Ma?" BJ spoke looking into his mother's eyes. Liyah quickly ran over and kneeled down beside the two.

"Did yall kill that muthafucka?" BJ asked causing Cash and Liyah to laugh.

"Yes, he's dead."

"Good. because on my little brother grave I was gone haunt that nigga until I found him.' BJ's lips curled with anger.

"Liyah call an ambulance." Cash shouted, noticing BJ was shot.

"Where are you hit at?"

"My side and my leg right by my dick. Ma tell them muthafuckas hurry, I can't lose my dick."

"Oh my god boy." Liyah and Cash both laughed.

"You're gonna be alright son, you and yo dick." Cash laughed.

Thirty minutes later, the ambulance arrived along with the police. The ambulance quickly put Papi onto the stretcher and rolled him to the ambulance.

Liyah watched with nonstop tears. She tried to imagine life with out BJ but couldn't. She loved BJ to death so she prayed he would be okay. She wanted to raise her family and she needed BJ here with her and her unborn child.

"We have another body inside!" an officer yelled out.

"Liy Liy go with BJ." Cash told her with a serious look.

"Ma'am are you responsible for the gunshot victim on the yacht?"

"Yes." Cash nodded and looked at Liyah.

Liyah walked off towards the ambulance to ride to the hospital with BJ. it was like a fresh pair of tears came cascading down her face because she didnt want to leave Cash.

As the ambulance doors were closing, Liyah looked at Cash who sat in the backseat of a patrol car, and mouth the words. *I love you mom.* Making Cash smile. Cash watched as the ambulance pulled off. She said a prayer for BJ then one thanking God for Liyah. Had Liyah not showed up in time, she was more than sure Que would have killed her. *I don't know when, I don't know how, but my daughter turned into a straight fucking savage in the blink of an eye.* Were Cash's thoughts as the patrol car slowly pulled off.

THE END!

Epilogue

a year later….

(Monique) "superior court of Miami, Vs Monique Moore Case number BA662019011 we the jury find the defendant, Monique Moore, Guilty of 1st degree murder."

I sat in the courtroom before all these white people, and my life had just been taken from me. I looked around at all the jury's and it was only one black. I figured he was my only chance to at least a hung jury but I thought wrong. My body was so numb that I couldn't even cry. I was straight framed for something I didn't do. This shit was crazy. Someone planted a gun on me which was the main reason I was convicted. Not to mention, the text messages found in my phone cursing Papi out about his new little bitch, was used against me as evidence. The DA's motive was jealousy. I had a dump truck ass public defender, that didn't even fight for me. Thanks to my so called daughter, I couldn't get a paid lawyer. I tried reaching out to Papi but all he ever did was laugh. One time he came and put some money on my books. Imagine my surprise when they told me I had six whole dollars on my books.

The least person that I had expected, stood up to the plate; Arcelie. She was at every court date and even put money on my books. After she came to see me the other day, I told her continue to run my salon so I could get money during my stay. My PD told me in about five years, I would go up for an appeal, which was my only hope. I came to realization, that my life had finally caught up to me, and I guess this is what God had in store for me. You could bet your last dollar, that I wasn't gonna stop. I was gonna be back on the streets and I swear, everyone would feel my pain; even Kamela backstabbing ass.

(Kamela) Life was good. I moved to Cali, and might I add, this was the best choice over any states. They had some fine ass niggas here, lots of ballers and even tricks. Every weekend I hit clubs in hollywood and, not, one soul knew of me. Thanks to Monique's money, I was out here living like a baller, popping bottles in clubs, driving foreign cars and wearing the hottest gear. The money I had was pretty much stashed away. Thanks to my new ass and double D tits, these niggas was in love and paid my way. I was on my shit looking like them girls on instagram. Call me fake if you want, but my body slamming, which is why I'm paid now.

I know what y'all thinkin, I'm a scandalous bitch for running off on Monique, but hey, I got it honest. Her Karma had finally caught up to her. She was never a good parent to me, her ass just fake the funk. That bitch hated me just as much as I hated her and its been that way. All she gave a fuck about was herself and whatever nigga was between her legs. When she fucked Papi and pretty much snatched him from under my nose, was the last straw. That nigga was my meal ticket but thanks to Hoe'nique, she ruined it for me.

I had no plans on going back to Miami. I started my new life, and I was happy here away from everyone and their drama. I changed my number because my dad was blowing my shit up. When I received a text from him that said *Yo ass something else. Good job ma. Lol. just be safe and trust me we will meet again* I couldn't stop laughing. He hated her just as much as me, and that's why I chose to live with him. Today I had a meeting with Author Barbie Scott. She's gonna write my life story, and boy I had a lot to tell.

(Braxton) its been an entire year since Cash left me and I was distraught. After all I've done for her she chose the thug over me. Since the first time I found out about Ms. Cash Lopez, I'd been in love with her. The day I took her from the hospital, I was determined to make her mines. I knew making her falling in love with me would be a mission, because of the types of guys she always dealt with, but I still played my hand. I always thought that her giving me my first child would at least make us bond, but that to was a complete lie. Every time we made love, I knew she was thinking of her husband, because she had called me his name on many occasions. I knew she missed him dearly, so I didnt really care. I had her in my presence, laying next to me every night, so there was no need to be jealous.

The day she kept Skylar from me, I didn't bother to go to the authorities. I knew what Cash was capable of so I didn't wanna risk my life. After about three months she brought Sky to visit, then the visits turned into a normal routine. She began to come every month and stay for at least two days so I could bond with my child. On one particular visit, we actually made love, which shocked the hell out of me. I knew deep down inside she only made love to me out of guilt, and because I was pretty much obsessed with her, I allowed it. No matter what, I'll never stop loving Cash Lopez and I'll be right here waiting for her every return. Trust me, her love affair with the thug won't last long, so I'll be here to pick up the pieces. Call me crazy, but I'm a man in love and one thing I know, is women like Cash Lopez only comes once in a lifetime.

(Kellz) a nigga couldn't be more happier with life. I finally got to be with my kids, because they bitter ass momma finally accepted the fact that we were done. At times, I felt like I was making a bad decision, but everyday Cash proved me wrong. We were thick as thieves, except for the one trip every month she took to her punk ass baby daddy house. I swear if I ever found out she was giving that nigga my pussy, Im bury both they ass in Forest Lawn Cemetery. I sacrificed so much to be with Cash so I'd be damned if she played a nigga.

The night she had the run in with Que, a nigga was worried shitless. I was blowing up her phone but never got an answer. A part of me thought her ass was somewhere getting ratchet, but the other part of me knew, that wasn't the case. If it was one thing I knew about Cash, was, her ass was gonna handle her business first and she wasn't gonna stop until the shit was handled.

Imagine my surprise when I got a call from MPD to pick her up. I would go into details but Ima let her tell yall that part.

I fully turned over the restaurant's back to Cash and Papi and was now focusing on my laundromats. I was in the process of opening up a movie theater called Brooklyn Cinema and I couldn't wait. Despite me fuckig with Cash, I missed the fuck out my dog. I always thought back to our conversation and laughed every time.

"Something ever happen to a nigga, I need you to be there for my girl."

"What you mean nigga?"

"Like be there for her. I'm not saying marry her or nothing, but shit if you gotta marry her, do it. I don't want no new nigga around my seed Kellz."

"Ha ha ha, man you crazy as hell nigga. So you telling me you want me to wife your wife?"

"Shit if that's how you put it. I dont trust nobody with her, or my businesses."

"I feel you but nigga that's crazy." we both laughed.

I wanted to tell Cash about that conversation so bad, but I didnt want her tripping. I knew Cash like a book, and her ass would probably dig Nino up just to kick his ass then bury him again, so I left it alone.

On another note, Its crazy how in one year, Cash made me happier than my wife in 16 years. I loved the ground that girl walked on, and I wouldn't trade her for the world. Couldn't no bitch in the state of Florida fuck with Cash and that's how it's been, and would always be.

(Breelah) Just when I thought my life was complete, everything turned upside down in a matter of days. Yes I loved Que, and yes this shit was paining me, but for some reason I couldn't put my whole heart into the nigga. Something about him was off. The way we talked, and the way he acted, let me know he was hiding something. Everyone that knew Que, just as I knew Que, know what I mean when I say, that nigga was always into some shit.

Knowing he had my brother killed a second time, was tormenting. But what really got me was the explosion. He didnt even care that I was on the ship. He just blew the muthafucka up, leaving us all to die. Fuck me, fuck Cash and most of all, fuck the kids that were aboard. That nigga had lost his everlasting mind.

Oh lets not forget the part of him being a fucking snitch. When Cash told me about that, that shit blew me back. He was the most solid nigga from the empire in my eyes, but I guess I thought wrong.

Just thinking on the past, It all began to make sense. He was head over heels in love with Cash, but that was all a front. He wanted to get close to her so he could take over the empire. *Cold nigga.* I swear he did a great job at acting, because he sure had me convinced.

Now here I am, back to square one. No man, no kids and my stressful ass job. The way Que made me feel, hell, I didn't trust any man and I know that's how it would be for a long time.

I tried to move out the mansion, but Cash nearly lost it, so I stayed. I didn't mind, long as she didn't mind. I enjoyed our family, shit they were all I had. Papi and Liyah had a son, and Cash and Kellz were doing great. I knew sooner or later I would want to find love, but right now I had to work on myself.

(Papi) I never thought in a million years, I would be a father. Liyah had gave birth to my first baby boy. Weighing in at 7 pounds and 11 ounces, he was a split image of a nigga. I wanted so bad to name him Brooklyn the third, but because he didn't have my middle name, he wasnt considered a jr. However, we did name him *Escolan Brooklyn Carter* after my dad and grandpa Esco. Right now he was six months old and already he was getting into shit. He ran around in his walker like the tasmanian devil. My mom always said he was just like me in many ways, I just prayed he wouldn't be when he got older.

In just these few short years of my existence, I had already seen and experienced to much for a nigga my age. The shit, I've seen, and conquered, I didn't want Lil Sco to have to deal with that shit. Now that we had eliminated all our enemies, I was more than sure we could go on with our lives.

My club was doing great and not to mention the money I was investing into Aaliyah's club, we were gonna be straight for the rest of our lives. Liyah had her own dough, but it was my job to cater to her every need. I don't know what it is about her, but its like she changed overnight. She had two bodies under her belt and now she was walking around like she was Columbiana or some damn body. Lately I had been contemplating asking her to marry me, but I don't know man, she was moving to a different tune. I mean don't get me wrong, we were happy, and always enjoying life, but something about her was off. In due time, I was gonna pop the question though, because this girl was really my soulmate.

Life was good besides Liyah ol Griselda Blanco head ass. My moms was happy with her new love life, and my little sister love that nigga Kellz, so that was all that mattered. I felt kinda bad for my aunt, because she was back to square one. I know she was on her *fuck niggas* tip after Que, but the way Young was checking for her, I don't know, her ass might bite. To be honest, I hope she do because Young was cool ass fuck. It wasnt too many people I trusted, but Young was one. Shit everybody needs love, and I finally realized that. Even Cali and Venicia were working on their family. At first Venicia wasn't fucking with that nigga, but she finally came around. They had a baby boy also that they named Cali.

Right now we all sat by the pool as Kellz Barbecued. Shit been peaceful with my family, and I prayed it would stay like that. I was still the man of these streets, a true *Trap Boy* by nature, and no one could knock me off my throne.

(Cash Lopez) "Boyyyyy" this has been a long year. A good one but long. I had the best man God could give me, well next to Brooklyn Nino. Can't no man on earth take Brook's place and I'm sure they all knew that. Kellz was good to me though and with him I was secure. It was like, I was the storm because of all the things I've been through, and he was my calm. The day he chose me over a woman he had been with since school, proved to me he was the one. He had finally gotten a divorce, and to my surprise his ex wife wasn't tripping. She let her kids come over on the weekends, and all though we didn't speak, she wasnt a pain in my ass. A few times Kellz had mentioned kids, but no way was I bringing another baby into this world. I had Lil Esco and Lil Cali so I was good on kids. Lil Esco was a hand full. I swear he was like another reincarnated BJ. At only six months, this little boy got into everything. Every since his mom had killed Camery and Que, her ass was on some gangsta shit. It was really crazy because she reminded me so much of me. However, I pray she didn't follow in my footsteps. Lately she had been asking me all kinds of questions about killing and drugs, and that was a sign of interest. *Lord have mercy.*

Braxton and I had finally came to terms because of our child. I made sure to take Sky to see him monthly because I wanted them to keep the bond they always had. I asked him plenty of times to move down to Miami but he would always refuse. A few times I had went to visit, I slept with him out of guilt. One drunk night, and heavy thoughts, led me into his bed; I just prayed he would never tell on me. I loved Kellz so much. If Braxton told, I would probably kill him. I couldn't, and I refused to lose Kelly. Kelly and I were opening a movie theater and it was the best idea yet. When he decided to name it after Brooklyn, that shit warmed my heart. I know deep down inside he didnt mean for us to fall in love but who better than the only man Brooklyn trusted that would keep me secure.

Life was great due to all my enemies being eliminated. Mario was finally gone, and the nigga that I always thought I could trust, was now dead and gone. I couldn't believe Que. This whole time he was the one that set my mom up to go to jail. I could just imagine shes prolly rolling over in her grave. The nigga even worked with Mike, now that's even crazier. I think it hurt me more to know he was a snitch. Even more than knowing he was behind the explosion. If it was one thing I hated, and that was a fucking rat. I hated I couldn't be the one to kill him, but knowing his own flesh and blood pulled the trigger, was the satisfaction I needed. When I was taken down to the station, they questioned me about Que being murdered. Of course when I gave them my name, I was quickly released. They ruled the murder as, trespassing and self defense, especially because BJ was shot and on his own yacht.

Last night I had a long talk with Liyah and she looked like she wanted to ask me something. I was more than sure it was the question she's been dying to ask. *Did I kill her mother?* For some odd reason she didn't ask, but when she did, I was gonna be truthful.

Well y'all, its been a long ride and guess what? Cash muthafucking Lopez in back in the flesh and still the baddest bitch around. My whip game still cold over the stove and I got the purest shit on the streets. You damn right, I copped three hundred birds and, THE BITCH IS BACK! Grade A *Trap Gyrl*

(Aaliyah) the night my Apa was killed by Cash, I didn't regret shit. When I killed Que, I didn't regret shit. When I pulled the trigger on Camery, and sent Monique dumb ass to jail, I didn't regret that shit either. All my life everyone thought that I was the sweet innocent little Liyah, but what they failed to realize, was, I was raised by my grandfather who was the coldest killer in Miami. My entire life involved death. Not one person in my family died from natural cause because everyone died from the hands of another killer, so I had it in me to begin with.

I wanted so bad to ask Cash about my mother's death but I chose to leave it alone. I knew one day the subject would come up and you know what? I wouldn't even be mad at the outcome. I've grown to know the real Cash Lopez and everything she did had a meaning. It didn't take a rocket scientist to know she killed my mom because the demis my grandfather caused. Shit, he killed her whole family. Just because Que blew up the ship physically, Mario ass was behind the hit, so those people's blood was on his hands.

I tried my hardest to stray away from the person that I was now becoming. Because of my son, I didn't want this life but everyday it pulled me in. I was trying hard to just focus on my strip club but it was something about the way Cash looked over that stove, that was tempting me. She was really my idol and it felt like I was transforming into her. The stories she had told me, always had my undivided attention. It was like, I wanted to be Cash, and she was now my *Ms. Lopez.*

She, and my grandfather were fucking millionaires due to selling coke. They both sold drugs all over the state and never had a run in with the law. Papi told me I was crazy, but that nigga had his fucking nerves. True, I loved Papi to death but he had put me through so much; I had a wall up between us. Right now it was all about me and these fantasies of being a Boss Bitch. The thought of selling drugs weighed heavy on me, and It was like I had gotten an adrenaline rush from the murders I committed. So here I am, on a rise to come up. Hey, you never know, I might just be the next Trap Gyrl, or should I say, *TRAP PRINCESS* (wink).

I just wanna say THANK YOU to all my supporters. I almost ended the Trap Gyrl sequel at part 3 but I couldn't leave yall hanging. I hope yall enjoyed this novel and it doesn't stop here. Well at least not the *Trap* title. But say bye bye to Cash Lopez because she's done everything. What else could she do? Lol

Thank You Cousin, Takiya Phillips.. I Love You!

Thank you again to Vanessa & Skylar :) I love you ladies and thank you guys for everything.

Thank you C Miller (aka) Pokelezy for dealing with my late night calls about what part I'm on. You always take time out yo day to bug me about what part I'm on, and that motivates me more.

My supporters I love yall for real. :)

Make sure you guys leave a review on amazon and also read A Thugs Worth…

Free Dajah Sutton… I love you niece. Make sure you pass this book around the jail lol I'm waiting on your arrival. 1,000 kisses :*

My mom(Toni) sister (Chunks) and nieces (Lay Lay, Miya and Cali) I love you guys to death.
My husband (Bugsy) and kids (Blessyn & D'Anthony) I love you guys and thank you for allowing me the time to write.
My baby girl Chastity, I could write a paragraph but Ima keep it simple. I love you my Trap Princess just don't get any ideas. (wink)

CPSIA information can be obtained
at www.ICGtesting.com
Printed in the USA
LVHW051604120419
613989LV00020B/424

9 781723 58522